D0831113

Also by James Albany

Warrior Caste

Mailed Fist

James Albany
Mailed Fist

SEVERN HOUSE

This first U.K. hardcover edition published 1983 by
SEVERN HOUSE PUBLISHERS LTD, of
4 Brook Street, London W1Y 1AA
with acknowledgement to Pan Books Ltd

ISBN 0 7278 0870 2

Printed in Great Britain by The Anchor Press Ltd
and bound by Wm Brendon & Son Ltd
both of Tiptree, Essex

Contents

1 Enter the hunters

Extract from the War Diary of Generalmajor Erich Münke

By November 1942, Generalfeldmarschall von Kleist believed that Russia was already lost to us. He had asked for permission to withdraw the army but had been refused. It was not danger that angered him so much as waste. Von Kleist, of course, was more of a patriot than he was a Nazi, just an old hussar at heart. So gut-sick was he of broken promises that I believe he would have been willing to exchange his panzergruppe *for fifty armed horsemen and lead a final charge across the Don just to be finished with that damned fizzling Caucasian campaign. When the freeze came and the mud turned tankable, however, I imagined that von Kleist would find fire rekindled in his belly and would stop quoting, sarcastically, the Führer's 21st Directive, a document sadly tarnished by historical events: 'The bulk of the Russian Army is to be destroyed in daring operations by driving four deep wedges with the tanks, and the retreat of the enemy's armed forces into the empty regions of Russia is to be prevented.'*

Simple enough: indeed, if the General Staff had not cast its shadow between intention and act Russia would have been ours by the end of the summer.

As it was, nothing had gone according to plan and the Führer himself had taken over complete responsibility for strategy. Small wonder that von Kleist was embittered by the failure of the summer campaign.

In the beginning how could any of us have guessed that Russian quantity would surpass German quality? But such a quantity! Six million Russians dead in six months: and still they marched out of the tundra to die on the banks of the Volga or in the blood-red streets of Stalingrad.

Von Kleist once told me that he felt the Führer would be more comfortable playing with wooden horsemen than with

armoured divisions. While I was careful, as a mere
Generalmajor, to express no positive opinion on that score I
did tend to agree with him.

Perhaps that is hindsight.

Even at the time, though, it was obvious that the summer's
fast running was behind us and that our cutting edge had been
blunted by over-conservative policies and lack of adequate
supplies.

Soviet prizes would not fall to us like snowflakes after all.
Even the oilfields of the Caspian, which lay tantalizingly close,
were protected by high mountains, winter weather and the
partisans. Yet that November morning, when I saw sunlight
strike the snows of the pass above Roshtan for the first time,
I felt a surge of confidence and an eager anticipation of the
fight.

We had tradition on our side, we of the Edelweiss divisions.
Had not the Gebirgsjäger scaled the heights of Mount Olympus
and gained the summit of Mount Elbruz because the Führer
wished it? Now my orders were to capture and secure the high
pass of Baku-Ashran. I had no fear of the mission. The terrain
was perfect for the men of Gebirgsjäger 88, my hunters of the
snow.

Roshtan, a small mountain village held by partisans, was
the key to the pass three thousand feet above. From the saddle
one could discern the black smoke of oil refineries far away
across the plain, and on a clear day, through a powerful
telescope, make out the derricks – so I had heard. I hoped that
tomorrow would be fine so that the boys might enjoy the view.

Night frost had turned the earth to asphalt. Panzer units
had rutted the track badly and there had been nothing but a
little surface thaw. We travelled briskly, though, and
approached the grouping base several hours before we were
expected.

I halted my command car. I got out, positioned myself on
a knoll by the roadside and waved to the boys as they tightened
the column; four six-tonners, four gun-tracks, then the
Kettenrads, horse wagons and foot soldiers. In spite of a

three-day trek from the railhead at Kareva the boys were as fresh as paint and held their heads high as they came to the mark. The peaks of their Bergmütze were pushed jauntily back from their faces but otherwise they were as military a bunch of lads as one would find anywhere. Happy to be out of the foothills' drizzle, stimulated by the clean, sharp air of the mountains, they shouted as I saluted them.

Tomorrow it would be our turn to make war. Some of my lads would die, no doubt, but they would die bravely in the white snow – which was all that a Jäger asked for, and the only favour he expected.

I climbed back into the command car and proudly led the 88th into the hamlet of Dzera where Gord's SS Panzer Corps was leaguered.

It was truly a magnificent afternoon, the sky blue, the mountains soaring under spotless mantles. My troopers sang lustily as we approached the line of tanks.

Dzera stood at the mouth of a narrow side valley. It comprised only a few stone cottages and the shrine of some wild saint whose blessing was required, so legend said, for a safe passage across the Baku-Ashran. A few small coins would have been enough. Perhaps I would have even made the gesture. But SS-Oberführer Gord had got there before me.

Gord did not believe in token propitiation, however; he preferred sacrifice.

Seventeen men were hanging from a scaffold that Gord's pioneers had erected. They had been stripped naked and used for pistol practice. In the sunshine, blood from their wounds had thawed out and dripped now, like burgundy, down their naked limbs.

Behind me the songs of the Edelweiss ceased.

SS-Oberführer Gord emerged from the church in which he had set up his corps HQ, and strode forward to greet me. He was accompanied by his henchmen, captains Wandsdorf and Schenken.

They saluted: Heil Hitler!

*I got out of the car and formally returned their salutes.
My sergeants brought the boys to a halt. I could hear their
mutterings at the sight of the bodies, every eye drawn to the
scaffold on the rise of the hill at the end of Dzera's cobbled
street.*

*'You have made excellent time, Herr Generalmajor,' Gord
said. 'You are to be congratulated.'*

*'Who are these men?' I did not beat about the bush. 'And
why were they executed?'*

*'They were partisans. To be more accurate, gun-runners.
They were caught yesterday evening. Red-handed.'*

'Were they questioned?'

'Of course,' Gord answered.

*I did not like the Oberführer much. He was excessively
handsome, with a tapered waist that made his uniform look as
if it had been tailored by Donner's of Berlin. He had pale skin
that had taken no lick of sun and very large, almost feminine
eyes, more green than blue. He was, I judged, about twenty-
eight years old which seemed to me, at forty-four, indecently
young for a major-general.*

'What did they tell you?' I said.

'Precious little, Herr Generalmajor.'

'When did you execute them?'

'At first light this morning.'

*'Would it not have been more prudent, Gord, to await my
arrival?'*

'They were our *prisoners, Münke, prisoners of Waffen-SS
Panzer Group Eleven. My responsibility.'*

I turned my back on the hanged men.

'Why have you left them there?'

'As an object-lesson to other partisans, Herr Generalmajor.'

*'It is – insanitary to leave them, Herr Oberführer. Have
them cut down and buried, if you please.'*

*We were equal in rank and, to be frank, neither of us
was quite certain who was in command of the joint operation.*

*It was typical of the Führer to omit this valuable detail from
his radio briefing. Perhaps he intended that we would do our*

*jobs in a spirit of amicable cooperations; a difficult matter
when one is dealing with the Waffen-SS.*

*I signalled to my senior officer who climbed out of the
Kettenrads in which he had been travelling. I issued instructions
for the feeding of my boys. As the panzers had already claimed
the habitable buildings, a piece of ground had been cleared
and staked out for our mountain tents, and a separate field-
kitchen set up. Great tubs of soup and stew simmered under the
awning.*

*The panzers' tanks and light artillery had been dispersed
and camouflaged, sentries posted.*

*Beyond the scaffold, where the mountain road began, two
gun emplacements had been established: 15 cm SIG 33 field
guns, under snow capes, flanked by MGs and mortars. It
looked, I must admit, as if Gord's unit had been here for a
month, not just a couple of days. It also looked as if the
SS-Oberführer had dug in rather too thoroughly for an advance
column. I had been told that we would encounter no regular
military opposition, only groups of partisans, widely scattered
and ill-equipped.*

*We entered the HQ that Gord had established within the
church of Saint Demetrius. I was pleased to note that at least
my SS colleague had not stripped the walls of icons to use
for fuel and had had sufficient respect for a religion in which he
did not believe to cover the rude wooden altar with a couple of
army blankets. A portable wood-stove had been installed in
the priest's cubicle and radio operators stationed in the crypt.
The church had no spire, but the village watch-tower,
decapitated by a stray shell, stood in the yard behind it,
built up on a stone barn. A slit window, devoid of glass, provided
a framed view up the high winding track to the summit of the
pass.*

*I was given tea, a black bread and salt-meat sandwich, for
which I was grateful. But food did not appease my disgust at
the wanton slaughter of the peasants, even if they were, as
Gord claimed, part of the partisan army. I felt then that these
people were entitled to defend their homes and homeland and*

11

that as they were not spies they did not deserve to die brutally on a rope's end.

Personal sentiments apart, I was annoyed at Gord for having tipped our hand. The Edelweiss had been sent in to fight, mountaineer against mountaineer, and the Waffen-SS had made that next to impossible. It was patently obvious that the seventeen prisoners had been tortured. I could imagine their screams echoing in the high mountains, a rallying call to every uncommitted peasant in the sector.

Frankly, looking back on the events of that week, I lay the blame for what happened squarely on Gord's shoulders. For a start, the SS-Oberführer did not obey my order to have the bodies cut down: he left them just where they were, dangling from the goalpost scaffold like crows on a fence.

And that, as it turned out, was a bad mistake.

However, at the time, I was preoccupied with finalizing a plan for the morning's attack. It was my intention to capture Roshtan soon after daylight. Gord's intelligence sources indicated that no more than four hundred partisans defended the village, though reinforcements had been summoned from regions to the north. The fast-running panzergruppe and our rapid arrival from the railhead had, however, caught the Roshtan brigade unprepared and under-strength for repulsion of a full-scale military assault.

If the Führer's 21st Directive was not only obsolete but rather a joke. Directive 45, by means of which the 4th Panzer Army had been pulled out of Stalingrad to boost the armoured assault on the Caucasian oilfields, was a serious miscalculation. In July and August everything had looked so auspicious. Now, in November, there was no impetus left in the Southern Army's thrust, only, effectively, us: Panzers and Jägers – a mailed fist on a withered arm. Even so, if we could punch through the bastion of the mountains, open and hold the pass of Baku-Ashran, the Soviets could not possibly defend the remote Caspian cities in the face of determined onslaught.

It was, as both Gord and I were aware, a campaign of the utmost importance to the Reich.

The plan came to this: the storming of Roshtan would be effected by a surprise pincer attack, preceded by two hours of heavy shelling. Gord's panzers would conduct a barrage lasting from one hour before dawn until one hour after. Ten units of the Edelweiss's best climbers, in two separate groups, would move under cover of darkness. With great stealth they would ascend the mountain ridges that flanked Roshtan to north and south. By dawn they would be in a commanding position above Roshtan. The partisans would hardly anticipate such a manoeuvre. Surprise and a superior position on the mountain would carry the victory.

If all went well, and we had no reason to suppose that it would not, we would be in possession of Roshtan by noon of the following day, Wednesday, and ready to make a final assault on the pass on Thursday.

I had a foolish vision of Roshtan being taken almost without bloodshed.

At the end of our tactical meeting I felt more kindly disposed towards SS-Oberführer Gord and walked out with him, in the last of the daylight, to inspect the batteries and muster my boys for briefing.

It was then that I saw again the line of corpses.

In the last stray rays of the setting sun the hanged men cast long shadows upon the blue snow.

I opened my mouth to reprimand Gord for not acceding to my wishes then thought better of it and accompanied the Oberführer, in silence, towards the gun positions.

Twenty minutes later, with the light almost gone and the valley filled with powdery shadow, we were summoned by a guard commander and hastened up the cobbled street to a forward post. There, behind a stand of baled hay and timber, sentries crouched, rifles and MGs trained on the road.

'What?' Gord demanded. 'What is it?'

'They carry a white flag, sir,' said the guard commander, pointing uphill.

13

'It's a trick,' said Gord. 'Open fire.'

'Sir, they are all women.'

Gord and I used our field-glasses. Even in poor light it was possible to make out the fact that the twelve peasants were indeed female.

They waved; the flag was a pale sheet knotted to a flail-pole.

'Shoot them,' said Gord.

'Wait,' I said.

'I know these people,' Gord said. 'Believe me, Münke, they aren't to be trusted.'

I ignored Gord and told the uncertain Scharführer to find a soldier who spoke Russian.

An Oberschütze claimed he could interpret. Hands cupped to mouth, the soldier bawled out questions.

The women replied in chorus, making a strange wailing sound that made the hairs on the nape of my neck prickle.

The snow gave the only real light now, though the mountains were well-defined against the satin sky. In Roshtan, four miles away and two thousand feet up, we could see the flames of cooking-fires dotted across the defence lines. After dark, for fear of air attack, the fires would be extinguished, of course.

'What do they say, soldier?' I asked.

The Oberschütze was puzzled. 'I think they said they want to die, sir.'

Gord laughed. 'Then we will oblige them, will we not, Münke?'

'Ask again,' I told the soldier.

He called out, his voice drawing echoes from the snows.

One woman answered. She had come forward from the group, which was some two hundred yards from us and well within range. The spokeswoman was tall and appeared younger than the others, though it was difficult to tell as all were bundled in drab woollens. Hands raised, the woman advanced down the track.

'Ach, sir, they want to take away the dead men,' said the Oberschütze, laughing. 'That is what it is. They want permission to remove their brothers and husbands.'

'If I thought they would be young and pretty,' said Gord, 'and if we did not have too much to do tonight, I would be tempted to charge them a certain old-fashioned price for the bodies. But we have no time to indulge ourselves. Shoot—'

'Hold the order, Scharführer,' I shouted.

I drew Gord to one side: it does not do for senior officers to squabble in public.

'What does it matter to us?' I said. 'You got nothing out of the men, did you? Nothing worthwhile. Our plans are made. We know all we need to know. Let the women take the bodies. It'll save us the trouble of burying them.'

'You do not know these people,' said Gord again. 'They are barbarians. I wouldn't be surprised if they want the corpses to cook for dinner.'

'Nevertheless, I am joint-commander here, Herr Oberführer. Unless you give me good reason for not obeying a simple law of humanity, I must insist that—'

Gord punched a gloved fist into the palm of his hand, the noise like a pistol-crack.

'Send out four men, Scharführer. Bring the bitches in three at a time,' snapped Gord.

'Thank you, Herr Oberführer,' I said, stiffly.

Although he had given in to me on this occasion it was obvious that Oberführer Gord and I had not had our last difference of opinion and that he would not capitulate so readily in future.

It did not occur to me then that I should have been more sympathetic towards that young major-general; he had been in Russia for thirteen long months and had fought through the bitterest of street fighting with the asphalt soldiers. Even so, I knew that the Waffen-SS considered themselves to be their own law-makers and tales about their cruelty were legendary.

The guards escorted the women to the scaffold at the head of the little street. The SS riflemen, I noticed, did not offer to assist the women in their grisly task. Two of the younger

15

women were obliged to hitch up their skirts and climb the icy posts and, with a knife provided for the purpose, cut the steel-hard ropes from which the corpses dangled.

An eerie silence had spread throughout the base. My boys, who had witnessed little of this sort of thing, had come out of their billets to watch the unusual happening. It resembled one of the ancient guild tableaux that used to be performed in remote villages in Bavaria.

A couple of pine torches lit the scene. I could smell the acrid odour of the burning pitch. The women moved cumbersomely, paying no heed to us or to the guards. Seventeen naked cadavers, twelve black-clad women, four riflemen, two major-generals, and a stunted street packed with curious soldiers: a queer cast indeed. Then, down the track, came a horse-wagon, a high-prowed cart typical of the region. I remember thinking that they would have been better with a log-sled. The cart was pulled by two large horses, its wheels roped to keep it from slipping on the freezing snow. The cart, too, was driven by a woman. Now that the sun had gone, the air was bitterly cold. I lifted my eyes to the mountains, thinking how well crampon points would bite into the snow tonight, how my boys would practically run up the ridges. The bodies were down, the horse-cart close; the Scharführer had just stepped forward to inspect it when all hell broke loose.

The first I knew of it was when SS Hauptsturmführer, Wandsdorf tackled me and flung me forcibly upon the snow.

A grenade exploded only twenty feet from where we lay.

Wandsdorf, poor fellow, was socked by a great chunk of ice. He grunted, reeled, and, rising to his knees, received a bullet full in the mouth. His face exploded in tatters.

I saw every vivid detail of his death, sprawled where he had flung me, by his knees.

Wandsdorf blubbered and collapsed and fainted away from me, a sticky tendril of blood hanging in the air where his head had been.

I rolled and reached for my side-arm but realized that I had

16

taken off my holster in HQ and had neglected to put it on
again. Defenceless, I crouched in the snow.

Gord was belly-down, ten yards from me. From the Luger
in his fist, he pumped shots into the cluster of women by the
scaffold. The pine torches had been extinguished, the signal,
perhaps, for the ambush to begin.

In the high-prowed cart was a machine-gun manned by two
round-headed, half-starved waifs of twelve or thirteen. They
were supported by an older lad with a sack from which he
plucked and hurled grenades in a whirl of movement like a
sower scattering seed. Shielded by the corpses, the mourners
produced guns. They had not been searched at the perimeter
but Gord's sergeant had paid for his negligence, shot four
times through the chest. The women fired a canister which
spread a curtain of thick brown smoke across the position.

Head down, I stayed put, watching the action out of the
tops of my eyes.

I had supposed that the women would snatch the corpses
and retreat in the cart. But Gord was right: I did not know
the Russians. The ferocity and courage of these tribes was
astonishing.

Thundering, the horse-cart came pounding on, while the
guards tried to recover and sweep their machine-guns round
to a new field of fire.

I would have been happy to crawl away if it had been
possible.

Smoke drifted towards me, reeking like burning thatch. I
heard the women shriek demonically, then they came too,
nine of them – three being already dead or wounded –
armed with blunt little tommy-guns, products of the local
arms industry. The home-made guns stuttered loudly in
uncontrolled bursts, short-range weapons, deadly at one
hundred yards.

Naturally, I had no notion of what was happening behind
me in the street. I guessed that there would be some measure
of panic even in the ranks of the Jäger. When I heard the first
tremendous explosion, however, I assumed that it was a panzer

17

gun, that one of the new Tiger tanks had swung quickly to the range; yet there was no flash, no whistling shell, no fountain of snow. A second explosion shook the ground. I had no time to take stock and retreat: the horse-cart was heading straight at me.

I rolled, rolled again, struck Wandsdorf's body, scrambled over it, flung myself into a bank of snow and pressed myself flat.

I cocked my head just in time to see the cart leap and the huge grey-white shapes of the draught-horses pass between Gord and me. All caution fled: I got to my feet and sprinted after the cart, hoping, somehow, to halt its deadly progress into Dzera.

To my right the Church of Saint Demetrius was illuminated by a fresh explosion. I felt rather than heard the blast, saw jetting flames only from a corner of my eye. I was running hard, without any particular purpose, towards the back of the cart.

By the law of averages I would surely have been mown down if the young grenade-thrower had not got in the way of the MGs muzzle. Then my team sergeant, Unterfeldwebel Scheibert, had the presence of mind to shoot one of the horses; a wonderful shot it was, straight through the animal's heart. The beast slumped dead in the shafts.

The cart tilted and rammed into the carcass. The second horse, terrified now that its forward momentum had been checked, reared against the traces and was instantly riddled with rifle bullets. The cart bucked and crashed over. The two little Russian gunners tumbled like acrobats in the air. The grenade-thrower dived towards me and slid on the thin snow that coated the cobbles.

I pounced on him: I wanted him alive.

I pinned his arms to the ground and stared into his broad, expressionless face. The ring-pin of a grenade was clenched in his teeth. The grenade – live – was clasped in his right hand. His eyes narrowed with amusement.

I swarmed away from him and, diving, covered my head with my arms. Twelve hundred metal fragments showered about

18

me. Why I was not wounded is a miracle, for I had covered only seven or eight yards before hitting the ground.

The young partisan was virtually blown apart.

I picked myself up and ran, not towards the buildings but into a clump of bushes by the gable of a cowshed, I crashed through them, scrambled over a mound of snow and, shouting in German, slithered behind the MG in our mortar pit. On the road up to Roshtan, however, there was not a partisan to be seen, except the bodies of the women who had been mown down at the scaffold.

Smoke had drifted away. I could look up the road, over the snowfields, to the prickle of camp-fire lights at Roshtan. Then I understood: the fires were decoys. The partisans had tricked us by striking unexpectedly and in force.

I told the guard commander to keep his eyes peeled, climbed over the snow wall and walked back into Dzera in search of Gord.

Gord, though white-lipped with fury, did not accuse me of stupidity to my face. Perhaps he would have been justified in doing so. His baggage had gone up with the church, a fact that seemed to enrage him even more than the loss of a quarter of our reserve fuel and six brand-new Tiger tanks. Mercifully the body-count was quite low: seven panzers dead and eleven wounded, two seriously. The Edelweiss had escaped unscathed.

Forty or fifty partisans, it was estimated, had attacked the leaguer from the rear, armed with triggered landmines, grenades and enough heavy explosive to blow us all to damnation. We retrieved some of their equipment but not one prisoner, not one live Russian.

As swiftly and silently as they had appeared, the raiders had slipped away again.

From the Russian viewpoint, it was a highly successful raid. We did not dare send out unprotected climbing parties that night and were obliged to waste a day revising our plans for the taking of Roshtan.

One day's grace was exactly what those Caucasian partisans

had hoped to gain; an extra twenty-four hours in which to fly in a squadron of the British Special Air Service and transform the taking of the high pass at Baku-Ashran into a fight to the death.

2 The devil in white

The Morris half-track tractor was the only one of its kind in captivity in the Middle East. Its acquisition by the Special Air Service had seemed like a good idea at the time. Fitted with a massive steel bow-plate, the machine served well at lower altitudes and coped adequately with the falls that sometimes closed the supply road below the ski school at the Cedars of Lebanon. Its thrust was monstrous, its rubber-jointed tracks seldom clogged or cracked, and Buz Campbell strenuously advocated its use in the search and rescue mission in the belief that it would save on legwork.

Four hours later, locked in a heavy drift and frozen to the bone, Buz cursed the bloody contraption blue-blind, and demanded to know whatever happened to mules as a basic form of transport in this God-blighted country.

'Sorry, this is as far as she goes, sarge,' said driver Jim Potter. 'I can back her down from here if I look nippy. But if I push on we'll probably lose her until the spring thaw, like Alf lost the truck.'

'All right, all right, goddamn it!' Campbell kicked open a floor locker and hauled out his pack, ski boots, goggles and overgloves. 'What a friggin' army!'

Deacon had already climbed out into the snow to off-load the skis.

'Give us a couple of minutes, Jim,' he called, 'and you can head for home.'

Sheltered by a flapping tarpaulin, Deacon carefully checked the ski bindings and clips. The going would be rough and a broken binding would be almost as serious as a broken leg.

When the Morris had finally roared itself hoarse and ceased to carve through the drift that hooded the bend, Deacon had taken a compass bearing and altimeter reading. He had calculated to within a quarter of a mile just how short of Trafalgar Square they were and what the extra effort of a slog across the high slopes might mean in terms of energy lost. It worried him less on his own account than on behalf of Buz Campbell and P. B. McNair whom he had selected to accompany him on the search.

The featureless landscape was obscured by winding sheets of snow, snow of various densities, from pellet-like granules to flakes as large as communion wafers. There was no accounting for it. Even weather experts, like Major Oram, were baffled by the sudden, swift changes of temperature in the Lebanese Alps.

Deacon's experience of high-level skiing, though considerable, had been limited to Switzerland and Austria and he had reckoned, wrongly, that the 10,000 feet high mountains of the Lebanon, pre-war playground of rich sportsmen from Beirut, Damascus, Haifa and Cairo, would be a piece of cake. After all he was, as Canadian Buz Campbell phrased it, a hot shot on wooden rods. It was true that he had studied skiing techniques on the Arlberg and had shot the downhill course at Engelberg in 1938 only a couple of seconds outside the best time of French champion James Couttet and, during the weeks of special training, had swanned it over the slopes like Alicia Markova with five o'clock shadow. Now, however, as the redoubtable Campbell was swift to point out, the chips were down and Deacon was surely obligated to lay his money where his ass was, to put into practice what he had preached.

Though rescue was a serious business the SAS would not risk the lives of trained soldiers needlessly, which was the principal reason why the party was limited to three.

Close to the summit of the Mountain of Baal, two SAS lieutenants had gone missing, which was bad enough. But with them was a Red Army colonel whom the Russians would not be exactly chuffed to have shipped home in a pine box.

Colonel Holms' instruction had been terse and very specific: 'Bring the beggars back alive, Deacon.'

Sergeant Buz Campbell and Corporal Peter Bennet McNair were not the best skiers in the outfit. They were, however, Deacon's mates. The three had fought side-by-side through half

22

a dozen desperate actions. Besides, Campbell and McNair had had the benefit of personal instruction in mountain survival and were physically and psychologically fitter than any man in the squadron.

Born and bred in a Glasgow slum, P. B. McNair had taken to skiing like a duck to water. Buz had done 'some crude stuff on the rods' as a boy back in Canada's Slocan Valley. They would need all their skills, however, to reach and return from the Mountain of Baal, for the big, bland summit had turned savage thanks to a three-day blizzard which showed no signs of having blown itself out.

The drift that blocked the track was layered like a cream cake, ice and floury snow packed hard by the winds that strafed the crest. The tractor's plate was embedded, the cab almost buried in spindrift before Deacon, Campbell and McNair, clamped up and saddled with rucksacks, were ready to strike out across the undulating sea of white. They would head diagonally upwards towards the ragged edge of the summit ridge, below which, before the blizzard, three tiny pup tents had marked the site of an overnight camp, a feature of the school's training programme.

'All set?'

'Yeah,' Buz answered. 'How about you, wee man?'

'Right as rain,' said P.B.

Deacon pounded on the cab door.

Driver Jim Potter wound down a window already plated with ice.

'Listen,' Potter said, 'where am I supposed to pick you up? Fat chance of getting up to Trafalgar Square now, sir. I could try to hold her here, if you like.'

'Too risky, Jim,' said Deacon. 'Besides, it'll take us the best part of the afternoon to reach the Ritz and, unless they're on the way down, we'll probably have to hole up until daylight tomorrow.'

'So what do I do about picking you up again?'

'Come up tomorrow morning. Look for us between here and the Round Pond.'

23

The landmarks, single stunted shrubs and summer pools, had been obliterated by heavy snow but officer and driver knew their general locations and the contours of the track were too familiar to be missed.

'Tell you what,' Potter suggested, 'I'll roll her up and down a bit to keep what we've got open.'

'Very well. But keep an eye on your fuel gauge,' said Deacon. 'Oh, by the way, tomorrow I suggest you bring along a medic.'

'Got you, captain.'

'On your horse, then, Jim.'

'Good luck!'

'Thanks,' said Deacon.

Campbell and McNair waited fifty yards along the clearway. Deacon drove his poles into the snow-cake and slithered down to them. Laden with equipment, the three SAS men herring-boned up the bank on to the virginal white slopes above. In silence they watched the tractor extricate itself from the drift and growl backwards down the channel it had carved out only minutes ago. Still in reverse, the Morris rounded a curve and vanished from sight.

'Goggles on,' said Deacon. 'And remember to keep pressure on your knees and not your ankles. We've a long climb ahead of us and I don't want a couple of cripples on my hands.'

'Right.'

Deacon led off across the mountainside. He adopted a rapid half-step technique, assisted by thrusts from the lower ski pole. Campbell and McNair copied him faithfully. Their packs, Norwegian jobs, hugged their bodies and awkward equipment – shovels and short-shaft axes – was buckled neatly in place. Even so, the weight of the packs disturbed their rhythm and progress across the fine, uncrusted snow was sluggish. After a quarter of a mile, Deacon was relieved to run on to a long, hard groove into which the skis' edges bit nicely and which encouraged him to swing upward and make height.

There was little point in searching for the Russian colonel's party on this line of approach. The truck had deposited the missing men at Trafalgar Square, a pile of boulders at the track's end. Radios weren't carried on training exercises and there was never more than one unit, three men in all, on the mountain at any one time. Stamina, self-reliance and mountain craft were on test and a time limit on the length of the exercise made it really tough, particularly as bad weather was deemed to be no excuse for tardiness. The current series of exercises, however, had an air of seriousness and of mystery, due to the presence of Red Army Colonel Boris Safaryan.

The regiment's finest mountain experts had been vacuumed up from the western deserts and disgorged at the school for extra training. Every man there was a veteran of raids against the Germans and more than a few had fought as commandos in Norway. There was no doubt that Colonel Holms was giving Safaryan the VIP treatment, though the Russian spent most of his time on the mountain, up to his crotch in snow, leading teams that struggled to meet the required standard of fitness.

But even the hardy Russian, it seemed, had come unstuck. His party was thirty-six hours overdue.

With the forecast offering no hope of an immediate break in the weather, Colonel Holms had decided to send out a search party. Deacon had been a natural choice for leader.

The pace that Jeff Deacon set across the breast of the Mountain of Baal would have exhausted most cross-country skiers within a half-hour. But SAS troopers were part of an élite group to whom the only standards that mattered were those they set themselves. P.B. and Buz trudged behind the captain without complaint. At least they didn't have to struggle with field weapons, and special-issue hooded snow-suits kept out the worst of the wind. Deacon broke trail. P.B., a small man, brought up the rear, protected by Campbell's bear-like bulk.

The groove of good snow frittered out in a trash of icy rocks where winds had laid bare the spine of the ridge. Deacon had no wish to resort to rope-climbing. He jumped around into the fall-line and swooped down three or four hundred feet, sacrificing height for position.

They had been forging upwards for two hours and still the

Summits of Baal seemed not one inch closer. The sky was an ugly blue-black, streaked with slate grey cloud. Odd to realize that hill villages only a few thousand feet below were probably basking in sunshine and that the afternoon in Beirut would be delightfully warm.

Deacon waited for Buz and P.B. to negotiate the little chute. P.B. had superb natural balance and maintained a vertical stance by forward inclination. Because of his size Campbell adopted a more defensive position on skis, crouched to decrease wind resistance. The pair *shushed* to a standstill beside the captain on a table of snow under the shelter of rock eaves. Deacon consulted the compass which hung from a cord about his neck, and took an altimeter reading. Impressions to the contrary, they had gained over a thousand feet in vertical height.

'Are we going up to the Basin?' Buz asked.

'Indeed we are,' Deacon answered.

They were only a half-mile north-west of the huge amphi-theatre – slung between the Mountain of Baal and Qurnat as Sawda's uninspiring 10,000 feet summit – that SAS trainees, with their customary love of the dramatic, had nicknamed 'The Basin of Satan'. As far as SAS troopers were concerned, the Basin was the trade route to the upper escarpments, a brutal uphill slog in one direction and a steep ski descent over bumpy terrain in the other, a section that severely tested a man's character and capabilities. That November afternoon, however, the lip of the Basin was festooned with fresh snow. Safe routes had been washed out by enormous drifts. Jagged *séracs*, splin-tered from the gullies, had been borne forward, like sentinels, on creeping avalanches.

Beyond the valley wall, Deacon detected the gun-metal glint of ice in the cleft of the Devil's Candlestick, the mountain's most hazardous ski-run, one which trainees were forbidden to attempt.

Deacon said, 'We'll skirt the lower part of the Basin and go in over the rib. Unless visibility deteriorates in the next couple of hours we should be able to spot them if they're in the Basin anywhere.'

P.B. – somehow – had contrived to light a cigarette. He pushed his goggles on to his brow and leaned nonchalantly against the rock as if it was a lamp-post at the corner of Argyll Street.

'They'd better no' be,' he remarked, nodding. 'Look't yon.'

Deacon and Campbell stared up into the bowl, watching the toppling *séracs* which fell, it seemed, in slow motion and with nothing but a plashing hiss, echoless and apparently harmless. Tons of coreless ice crumbled and bounded down and piled against the valley's nether rim, spewing mare's tails of fine snow into free fall.

'Jesus!' Campbell said.

'On second thoughts,' said Deacon, 'perhaps we should steer clear of the Basin altogether.'

'I'll second that motion,' Buz said. 'How do we go?'

'The long way,' Deacon answered.

'It figures,' said Buz.

Canting the uphill edges of his skis, Deacon set off, side-stepping directly across the fall-line.

The instability of the Basin and its vicinity worried him. If the Red colonel's party had been caught by one of the soft falls, their bodies would remain buried until the spring thaws. He wondered if Safaryan would be stupid enough to tackle the Basin in such conditions. Encounters with the ebullient colonel had not exactly filled Deacon with confidence. Safaryan was, as the Yanks put it, Gung-ho, too Gung-ho for his own good – or anybody else's. The colonel's brown Georgian eyes were lit with an inner fire that Deacon recognized as fanaticism. Only a fool or a fanatic would tackle the Basin of Satan under present conditions. Three days ago, of course, things may not have been so bad.

Grunting with effort, Deacon maintained a pure side-step until the slope eased a shade. He had gained sufficient height now to expose to view most of the great white bowl. He paused and had a look-see through his binoculars. The Basin leapt into focus. He saw the devastation that temperature changes had wrought. Major Oram would have been in his element; the bloody place was a casebook of lethal hazards. Of the Red colonel and two lieutenants there was no sign at all.

Stowing the binoculars, Deacon steeled himself for sustained effort and led off for the nape of the summit ridge.

The blizzard eased, then blew up again, flinging a dense grey curtain over the mountain for a while, then eased once more and dwindled, leaving the going difficult. Ski blades were fouled by greasy snow. As the angle steepened, work with the poles wearied the shoulders and back. Side-slipping strained thighs and calf muscles. Over the final four hundred feet of the ascent only will-power drove the three SAS men forward.

The light had begun to fade before Deacon hauled himself over the crown of the ridge and slid on to the strip of flat ground under the summit walls.

Protected by snow-cemented rocks, Deacon dropped involuntarily to his knees. Campbell sank to haunches and only P.B. seemed to have the strength to stay upright.

The Scot fumbled with the cap of a gill of Johnnie Walker and offered the bottle to the captain. Deacon accepted it and drank. Whisky numbed already numb lips, made his tongue and throat tingle, then trickled wonderfully down into his gut. He gave the bottle back and, restored, hoisted himself on to one knee and fished out the sectional map.

Buz squatted beside him.

'We're in Watling Street, right?'

'Yes,' Deacon replied. 'Only a quarter of a mile from the Ritz, where the tents should be.'

The map had been drawn by an SAS artist for the use of trainees. The mountain's main features had been given hospitable names. Watling Street, for instance, was a mile-long stretch of comparatively flat ground beneath the summit walls. It skirted the rim of the Basin of Satan and meandered into a dangerous area of broken rock at the top of the Devil's Candlestick. Big Ben, a prominent pinnacle, marked the site of the tents, the Ritz.

After six hours of hard ski-climbing it was tempting to rest but, by Deacon's reckoning, they had an hour at most in which to locate the missing unit and ensure that they were dug in for the night.

Pushing on swiftly, Deacon soon reached the spot where the tents should have been. He saw at once what had happened, how the cornice had come down on the tents and buried them. There was no trace of a camp there now, only a huge mound of snow. He dug his ski pole into it, thoughtfully.

'Are you thinking what I'm thinking?' Buz enquired.

'Probably,' said Deacon. 'I'm asking myself whether or not there's anybody under there.'

'Want us to probe?'

'What's the point?' said Deacon. 'If they were caught in the tents, they're dead for certain. We're a search-party, not a grave-yard detail. Besides, I don't much like the lie of the snow up there. We could have another slump at any moment.'

The cornice had already sprouted a new head, fresh snow streaked over the old stump. As the men stared upward, the carbon-black sky discharged a flurry of flakes and the shuffle of the wind across the summit ridge altered to a boom as its velocity increased.

Deacon said, 'We'll go on to the lip of the Basin and I'll fire a couple of flares. We'd better look sharp, though, get the signals off before the weather closes in again.'

'Jeff, I don't want to be a sourpuss, but we'll have to find a place to dig in pretty soon,' said Buz Campbell.

'Absolutely,' Deacon agreed. 'But not here. Building a snow hole anywhere under the summit ridge, with those wobbling cornices, would be asking for trouble. I imagine that the broken ground at the top of the Candlestick will offer the best protection. The drifts won't be too deep and the rocks are too jagged to hold a cornice, yet we'll be sheltered from the wind.'

Buz glanced again at the sky. 'The mercury's on the way down. We're in for a real ball-freezer, I guess.'

'You could be right, Buz.'

'Best move it.'

'Hoy!' P.B. jump-turned and slithered over to Deacon and Campbell. 'See what I found.'

'What the hell is it?' Buz asked.

P.B. held the object up at arm's length. Deacon took it, examined it, and shook his head.

'It's a special-issue overglove – with a mitten inside it.'

Buz frowned. 'Maybe some twit lost it last week or last month.'

'No,' Deacon said. 'It's soaked with blood, Buz, and still wet.'

'Found it there,' said P.B. 'just lyin'.'

'Uh-oh!' Buz exclaimed. 'Right by the snow pile.'

'Sound your whistle, Buz,' said Deacon.

'What about the cornices?'

'The air isn't sharp enough to cause vibration falls.'

Buz fished in his kangaroo pocket and brought out a wedge-shaped metal whistle. He tapped it against his thumb, put it to his lips and blew a series of piercing blasts. Pausing, he listened.

Holding the bloody glove between finger and thumb, like a talisman, Deacon scanned the length of Watling Street while the whistle's muffled echoes dwindled across the Basin.

'Again.'

Buz sounded another blast.

A knob of snow, large as a football, detached itself from the cornice two hundred feet above, plunged silently downward and exploded mushily into the snow mound, making the soldiers flinch.

'I'm beginning to like this situation less and less,' Deacon said. 'What the devil's going on? Freezing one moment, thawing the next.'

He stuffed the bloody glove into his parka pocket and skied along the ribbon of flat ground between hummocks of snow. P.B. and Buz followed him. Every fifty or sixty yards they paused while Buz rifled off another blast on the whistle and listened, in vain, for an answer. Below, in the Basin, the little *séracs* crashed wetly and gullies vomited a mixture of ice and slush, as if it was spring and not winter in the heights of Lebanon.

Watling Street narrowed. Deacon hugged the wall, preferring

30

to risk a fall from above rather than the trapdoor effect of unstable snow dropping him down into the Basin out of which, in such weird conditions, escape would be well-nigh impossible.

Squall winds reduced the whistle blasts to ineffectual piping. Buz put the whistle away and concentrated on holding himself in balance. The Basin yawned at his elbow, like something hungry. Darting sleet filled the air. Deacon worked quickly. Crouching against the rock he unslung his pack, took out a flare-pistol and unwrapped its waterproof cover. He fitted a cartridge, aimed the muzzle over the Basin and pulled the trigger.

The flare rocketed into space and, at the apex of its flight, burst into a red fireball which hung suspended for a moment then disintegrated and rapidly vanished.

Hands to mouth, Deacon cried the colonel's name.

'*Safaryan, Safaryan.*'

No answer.

The soldiers moved cautiously around the Basin's upper rim. Minutes later Deacon shot off a second flare and, with dwindling hope, watched it extinguish itself in the howling blizzard which had swooped over the blade of distant Qurnat as Sawda to engulf the Summits of Baal.

'You ask me,' Buz shouted, 'this is a friggin' lost cause.'

'We'll head for the top of the Candlestick. Be extra careful.'

'Don't worry.'

For the ten minutes that it took Deacon to navigate a route round the Basin's rim, visibility was reduced to zero, then, as suddenly as it had started, the squall billowed away. Cold crimped Deacon's skin. A patch of sky above the ridge of Qurnat as Sawda showed stars on a silken base. The clear air made Deacon even more anxious than the blizzard had done. If the night turned frosty the mountain would become a death-trap of steel-hard ice.

The jumbled rocks that marked the top of the gully in which the Candlestick began were silhouetted against an iridescent sky. In twenty minutes it would be full dark. Deacon set about searching for a suitable snow-bank in which they could hole up for the night. In the morning, early, he would exchange skis for crampons and comb the upper level from stem to stern. He was beginning to fear that the bloody glove had been torn off during a fatal fall, that the Red colonel and SAS Lieutenants Shipman and Hussey were buried somewhere in the broth-pot below.

The rime of sleet on his hood turned to ice.

He rammed his ski-stick into a shallow snow-bank on the lee side of a boulder.

'This will do. Buz, P.B., start digging. I'll give it one swift whirl and another flare.'

'Right.' Buz unstrapped his pack and removed the shovel.

Deacon left the NCOs to it and herring-boned up the snow by the side of the boulder.

Perched on the rock above, the thing resembled a gigantic predatory bird. The sound it made was like the cry of a hungry eagle. Its wings flapped and it descended on Deacon who – almost – ran it through with his ski-pole in a fit of irrational terror. Colonel Safaryan's white duffle jacket had been hung about his shoulders like a cloak. The colonel's shape, five-by-five and rotund, added to the illusion. In his excitement, the colonel had cried out in Russian.

On landing, upright, he reverted at once to his own brand of English while he hugged Deacon and danced.

'It was a run for me, morning. But you come in time. Ah, how pleased I am to greet you, my friend.'

'Colonel – are you injured?'

The colonel smelled strongly of sweat and sardines.

'Not Safaryan.' Pity wrote itself into the Russian's expression. 'Your Mike Hussey, he is wounded one.'

'And Shipman?'

'Shipman is dead.'

'Dear God!' said Deacon. 'What happened, sir?'

'Avalanche near top of Basin. Many stones. All of us sweep down. Mike Hussey, broken ski-pole into belly. Lung pierced too, maybe. Lieutenant Shipman,' the colonel tapped his brow, 'on head, here. Dead at once. Skull broke like egg. I bring Mike Hussey up to tents. But not safe. I bring him here and dig in. I go down again to look for Shipman. But he is dead.'

'Where's Hussey now?'

'Snow cave, I build. Two nights we are in there. What took so long for you?'

'Colonel Holms thought you might make it back on your own. We would have been here much earlier today, but the track—'

'Sure, sure.' Safaryan shrugged. 'I could not leave alone Mike Hussey or I would take skis down for help.'

'Is Hussey that bad?'

'Bad. Very bad.'

'Where's the snow-hole, sir?'

'Here, I show you.'

Deacon shouted to Buz and P.B. who joined them at once.

The three SAS men followed the colonel as he scrambled over a saddle of hard snow and picked his way between boulders to a narrow slit between two vee-shaped rocks. A khaki ground-sheet covered the opening. The snow-hole was large, though, and expertly constructed. Deacon rid himself of his skis and, leaving Campbell and P.B. outside, crawled through the groundsheet on Safaryan's heels.

The colonel lit a Metabrix tablet and the reek of the waxy fuel filled the cave. By the cooker's pale blue glow Deacon saw Lieutenant Mike Hussey laid out on a sleeping sack and wrapped in a groundsheet. Over the wounded man's face Safaryan had rigged a little awning to protect him from water drips.

'See. Bad.'

Mike Hussey, a couple of years younger than Deacon, had transferred to the SAS after a year's service with the Long Range Desert Group. Thin to start with, desert living had pared him down into a desiccated stick.

Conscious, he blinked at Deacon.

'Good God, it's the Deacon! Honoured, I'm sure.'

'Is it painful, Mike?' Deacon asked.

'Not too bad. But I'm damned if I'm riding down the hill on your back, old chap.'

Safaryan had bound Hussey's belly wound with strips of shirting. Deacon did not disturb the dressing. He didn't have to. The wet little wheeze in Hussey's chest told him that Safaryan's guess that the ski pole had pricked a lung was probably correct. Perspiration on the lieutenant's brow indicated a feverish condition, possibly – and not surprisingly – pneumonia.

Deacon understood Safaryan's predicament; how could the colonel leave a wounded man who, without care, would surely die? On the other hand, Hussey would die anyway unless he was pulled off the mountain and given expert medical attention very soon.

Deacon preceded Safaryan out of the cave again.

'How long has he got, colonel?'

Safaryan shrugged. 'He is tough as boots.'

'My guess – and it's only a guess – is that Mike won't last more than another twenty-four hours,' Deacon said.

'You ski good, captain?'

'Well enough, colonel.'

'We go down now, you and me. Tonight.'

'Yes,' said Deacon. 'But not you. Just me.'

'You break a leg – Mike Hussey dies. Two feet better than one, yes?'

'Are you fit enough? I mean, you've been three days—'

'Three days! Ha! I born in snow.'

'All right, sir. If we can reach Trafalgar Square before it turns dark, I'm sure we can find our way down the track. A full-scale rescue party, with stretcher and medical aid, could be on the mountain by first light. It's Mike Hussey's only chance.'

'The wee man and me, we'll stay and look after him,' said Buz.

'A thirty-man leap-frog,' said Deacon, 'should be able to get somebody up here by noon, in any sort of weather. They'll come up by the north-west ridge, as we did. Be on the look-out, Buz.'

'Are you goin' down the Candlestick?'

'Yes.'

'Holy shit!' Buz drew Deacon to one side. 'What's his nibs like on the rods?'

'I assume he's at least fair to middling.'

'What if he ain't?'

'Too bad.'

'You'll abandon him?'

'Naturally.'

'And he'll do the same to you?'

'Of course.'

'Goddamn it, Jeff—'

'Keep Hussey wrapped up,' Deacon interrupted. 'Don't give him any liquids.'

'Belly wound?'

'Yes, and lung too, probably.'

'I know how to handle it,' said Buz. 'Wee man, no smoking in the hole tonight, right?'

'Right, Buz,' said P.B. obediently.

Duffle jacket buttoned tightly about him and skis firmly clamped to his boots, Colonel Safaryan appeared by the mouth of the snow cave.

'Ready, captain?'

'When you are, colonel.'

'You have been down the route before?'

'After a fashion,' said Deacon.

'You lead?'

'By all means.'

'See you around, Jeff,' said Buz Campbell.

'No doubt about it,' Deacon answered.

Far below, daylight lingered on unbroken snows. No lights. Wintry mist, like sediment, covered the plains. The ski school buildings were hidden by the mountainside. No colour. When Deacon glanced down at his bright yellow ski gloves, their vividness startled him. He sighted the ski points towards the top of the gully, the Candlestick, and wondered what surprises it held in store. He had lied to Safaryan, of course; he had never skied the route before.

A preliminary traverse over wavy ground was ridiculously easy. He did not have to think about technique, merely let his body respond.

The skis gave off a pleasant sizzling hiss which told him that the snow was firm. Being shot of the back-pack made him feel extraordinarily light.

Cold air stung his cheeks. The sky over Qurnat as Sawda was liberally sprinkled with stars. He must not prejudge the level of difficulty or the run's dangers. He must take each section as it came, forget the glimpse he had had earlier in the day of gun-metal grey ice glinting in the gully. The rifling of the Candlestick was at its worst close to the end of the run. He would take it on the wing. He had no means of knowing what snow conditions would be like in any of the sections.

Linking a series of stem wedel turns, he ran faster.

Powdery snow billowed behind him like smoke.

Muscles, stiffened by the day's long climb, slackened.

He became more sensitive to the feel of the snow, to the increase in angle and the shudder of rutting where the snow pack had shifted across rock.

Rapidly now the gully's sides closed on him, graced with curves of blown snow.

Turning his head but not his shoulders, Deacon glanced back at Safaryan. The colonel, a natural squat skier by the look of it, dogged Deacon's tracks. The Russian emitted a strange yodelling cry to which Deacon did not respond.

The *piste* narrowed.

Deacon swallowed a mouthful of air and compressed his lips. He eased into a forward position, judging the moment of weight-shift accurately. His body action was smooth, steady, and he tried stem-swinging across the fall-line, short-radius swings that Safaryan, unless he was truly an expert, would not be able to emulate.

Suddenly Deacon realized that he was *competing* with the Russian. Absolutely incredible! But there it was. He couldn't help himself. On a run that was reputed to be a death-trap, he was showing off. Lieutenant Hussey was not uppermost in

36

his mind now, only putting on a quality show for the benefit of the Red colonel.

Deacon grinned at the revelation and risked making his stem-swings tighter still. No Russian peasant could possibly compete with the brand-new techniques that Deacon had learned, at considerable expense, in Switzerland.

He glanced round once more.

Safaryan was right behind him, stem-turning like mad, still yodelling.

And then the fun went out of it.

The Devil's Candlestick claimed all Deacon's attention. It was no longer a case of who was the better skier, but of who could survive.

Deacon's skis chattered on ribs of pure ice.

Stabbing lower edges and right-hand stick, he swayed out of the line. For a sickening moment he thought he had over-cooked it and was coming off. He stabbed again, counter-rotated, trying not to panic and rush the movement, settled, went down and forward on the outer ski, without allowing the inner to lift, and found within the gully bed a counter-ridge of sorts that enabled him to manufacture a braking swing.

The speed of the run was right on the limit of Deacon's control. He hoped to God that the Russian would manage to hold a similar line, would not wall-off on him and bring him down in a sweeping slide.

Ridged edge-downward plates of snow-ice disrupted Deacon's glide. He pressed his weight through his thighs and cut the plates deeply, braking further, then lifted in an un-expected jump, fluttered for an instant, and padded down.

Ground-waves flung him out of balance. He careered up-wards into the curve of the wall, sitting into it, hugged into an almost foetal posture that retained adhesion and shot him out like a rocket into the gully bed once more – and across it, banking him again until instinct took over and flexion thrust in his heels and pressure on the ski-edges was restored.

The gully walls seemed to be closing up completely.

A band of the night sky guided him as the run rifled into

its narrowest part. But Deacon had it now, had somehow accelerated his reflexes to cope with the speed. He took the long sweeping curve of the tunnel in a series of linked wedels, executed on the fall-line.

Coordination now was maximum and Deacon rode the twisting stem in a series of short diagonal side slips, shifting and flicking vigorously. Pendulum action of knees and hips and emphatic flexion gave him rebound. He felt the skis lighten, flatten. For several seconds he was nothing but a long, lithe strip of muscle magically attached to the skis.

Abruptly the gully walls fled.

Clear, dark sky winged out on either side of him.

Bulbous patches of soft snow below the gully mouth brought Deacon back to reality. He sprawled across the fan of the lower slope untidily, zigzagging lazily towards the spot where he thought the track might be.

He was still gliding light and easy when Safaryan whizzed past him with a maddening yodel of triumph and, crouched like a downhill racer, plunged over the edge of the drift and vanished into the piles of snow beneath.

It took Deacon five minutes to dig Safaryan out.

Five hours later, at a little after midnight, the Russian and the Englishman limped into the forecourt of the ski school and, shouting, roused Colonel Holms and the guard.

By one o'clock a.m., a party of thirty-six men had been mustered and equipped and were on their way, by truck and tractor, to assault the mountain and rescue Lieutenant Hussey.

When Deacon rose, well after the usual hour of reveille, he found that the storms had finally blown out and the sky was azure blue and the air crisp. He was stiff and ached in the legs but complied with discipline by ducking into a lukewarm bath before he dressed and went below in search of breakfast.

The mess was deserted but in the kitchen, the only really warm spot in the stone building, Safaryan had made himself comfortable and was doing justice to a couple of grilled chops that the cook had prepared for him.

Deacon wanted tea; tea and more tea.

'Sit here. We eat together,' said Safaryan, 'then we go out to help the others.'

'Yes, sir,' said Deacon, wondering if he had been given an order.

The cook put down bacon, dried egg and chops on a tin plate. Deacon found that he was hungry after all. He began to eat. The cook poured him a huge mug of tea. Deacon drank.

By now Safaryan had finished his meal. He sat opposite Deacon at the cook's table and smoked a cigarette, quizzical brown eyes scanning the young officer's face.

'You are son of an English lord, yes?'

Surprised, and a little embarrassed, Deacon answered defensively, 'Not exactly.'

Safaryan nodded and brushed his heavy brown moustache with his forefinger. 'Eton, Oxford?'

'Quite correct.'

'You work with Colonel Holms since Dunkirk?'

'Yes, before the formation of the SAS.'

'Sure, sure,' said Safaryan. 'I know all about you. Last night, before I go sleep, I read your dossier. It is very interesting.'

'Rather ordinary, really,' said Deacon. 'Lots of chaps in this outfit—'

Safaryan interrupted. 'Where you learn to ski so well?'

'Mostly in Austria and Switzerland.'

'On the Arlberg, maybe?'

'Why, yes, as a matter of fact.'

'I also. I train with Anton Seelos. You ever meet him?'

'Once or twice,' said Deacon.

Though he found the colonel boorish and suspected him of being a rustic peasant who had used the Red Army to climb into a higher social caste, Deacon had to admit that the fellow could ski. Even so, Safaryan had lost a man under his command, which was not a recommendation in Deacon's book. Safaryan might not have been guilty of foolhardiness on the mountain but Deacon was not disposed to give the colonel the benefit of the doubt. In due course, when sufficiently recovered, Mike Hussey would tell the whole story.

Deacon pretended to concentrate on his breakfast.

Safaryan, however, would not be deterred. 'You climb mountains also?'

'A bit.'

'More than a bit, I think, captain.'

'Sir,' said Deacon impatiently, 'is there a point to this cross-examination?'

Safaryan showed white even teeth in a grin. Reaching over the plates, he clapped Deacon on both shoulders. 'Deacon, my friend, you too modest. You brave man, I tell you. A very devil. The devil in white. I grateful to you. I do you favour, give you reward.'

Deacon stiffened. 'What sort of reward?'

'Tomorrow I take you with me to fight Germans in the Caucasus.'

'Thanks a million,' Deacon said.

3 Night of the big wind

Sergeant Buz Campbell was thoroughly pissed off with Operation Snowshoe long before the SAS combat detachment got within a thousand miles of the Caucasus. Throughout the ten hour truck ride from the ski school to the airfield at Masarat, Buz grumbled into the unheeding ear of P.B. McNair.

On arrival at the field, an outpost of Royal Air Force Middle East Command, the eighty hand-picked men of the combat party were given final briefing, told what they were expected to do and how they would do it; none of which soothed Buz one bit. After five hours of shut-eye in stuffy transit huts, and a meagre supper, the detachment was filed through the equipment sheds and thence to the waiting planes.

'Hell's Bells!' Buz complained. 'They ain't even Liberators. Take a squint at that goddamned museum.'

It seemed that No. 207 Group had not been terribly happy at being bossed about by a mad Russian even if he did bear signed orders from the Supreme Allied Commander, but they had grubbed about in the trash-cans of the Middle East Command and had come up with ten Whitley Mark V bombers, the type that Boris Safaryan had specifically requested. Whitleys were strong, reliable planes of sufficient range to make the drop and return to base without touching down to refuel in Turkey, a country whose neutrality the Red colonel trusted about as far as he could spit. No. 207 Group's mechanics had done a good job of converting the bombers into paratroop transporters and in tuning the old Rolls-Royce Merlin engines to stand the strain of a long, high-altitude flight.

'Why in hell do they need to drop us at all?' moaned Buz, as he manhandled his equipment up the short ladder into the plane's belly. 'Why can't they land us by the Caspian and mount an assault from there? It's only a couple of hundred miles inland to this village the Ruskie's so hot on hanging on to.'

'Buz,' said Deacon, 'will you please shut up.'

'I don't get it. I just don't get it.'

'You'll get it in the neck, sergeant, if you don't button your lip.'

'Right, all right.'

Buz knew perfectly well why a land assault was impractical. He had a good tactical brain when he chose to exercise it and had grasped the advantages of dumping the party, plus essential supplies, as close as possible to the mountain village.

On the south-eastern slopes of Baku-Ashran, the valley of the Ganevis river provided a perfect dropping zone. According to Safaryan, the river bed was frozen hard and comparatively free of major obstacles so that the drop need not be particularly tight. The SAS were not vastly experienced in parachute assault and had not yet developed the skills necessary for precision landings. In the wide valley of the Ganevis, however, assembly would be easy, leaving only a thirty-mile hike to the top of the pass to link with Safaryan's partisans. Local folk would be on hand to haul weapons and ammo to the summit, thus leaving the SAS free to make haste to Roshtan where, apparently, their presence was urgently required.

Buz wasn't stupid enough to denigrate the contribution that eighty trained soldiers could make to the defence of a mountain pass. The Red colonel wasn't the only one who had spotted the importance of that desolate route over the mountains.

The Mamison Pass had proved too difficult for the Axis to breach, and flanking moves through Nalchik in search of outlets to the Georgian and Ossetian highways had been blocked by Red Army patrols. Roshtan and the high pass at Baku-Ashran, which had at first seemed uninviting, had lately become the focal point of the German thrust into the oil-rich states. An un-expectedly well-organized switch of Waffen-SS panzers, the importation of crack Alpine troops, and an all-out effort at pushing dwindling supplies of fuel, food and equipment into Dzera had given the Russians no opportunity to regroup. Soviet regiments were, by then, heavily committed in other sectors. Since the winter's first snowfall on 18 September, Colonel Safaryan had been labouring to scrape up a defence of partisans,

42

armed peasants, anyone and everyone, including, at long last, a detachment of British Special Air Service donated by order of no less a person than Winston Churchill to whom Safaryan's personal plea had made enough sense for the PM to commit a few troops from a tiny regiment that nobody seemed to know what to do with.

In the past week, though, the Germans had accelerated their side-thrust and their primary objective had become obvious – Baku-Ashran. Colonel Safaryan had creamed what men he could from the Middle East Ski School and, only thirty-six hours after being rescued from the Mountain of Baal, was on his way back to Roshtan at the head of the raiding party.

The real reason for Sergeant Buz Campbell's intense dislike of Operation Snowshoe was the fact that the Caucasus was a long way from North Africa. Buz had been a desert raider for so long that he considered the Afrika Korps to be his personal enemy and the sandy wastes of Libya his battleground. He was proud of his record in the desert, proud of the SAS. He figured it was unfair to turn the squadron into cannon fodder just to appease the Ruskies. What's more, Safaryan's back-slapping heartiness turned the big Canadian right off. To some extent, against the facts he had gleaned from Lieutenant Hussey in the snow cave on the Mountain of Baal, Buz blamed Safaryan for Shipman's death.

What irked Buz most of all, however, was that nobody seemed to care how they were going to get back from Russia. During the briefing he had put that very question. The answer had been noncommittal, some crap about ferrying them out by boat from Baku. Nobody, Buz figured, expected them to come back at all.

Buz wasn't afraid of dying but he was fucked if he would die for some gung-ho Red colonel in defence of a mud-hut village in a foreign land. When the bell tolled for him he wanted to be buried in the hot dry sands of the desert, near the hulks of a convoy of kraut trucks or a train he had just blown up. When it came down to it, of course, he would prefer not to die at all.

'What the devil's wrong with you, Buz?' Deacon asked.

'I don't like it, I don't like any part of it.'

'It's just another mission,' Deacon tried to soothe him. 'A little more official than some we've been on but intrinsically the same.'

'Yeah?'

'We'll still be fighting Germans.'

'Yeah?'

'There will be plenty of action left for us in Tripolitani when we get back.'

'Let's say I just don't like snow.'

'Personally,' said Deacon, 'I prefer it to sand. At least it doesn't infiltrate your foreskin.'

Normally Buz would have laughed: he contented himself with a sullen grunt and Deacon left him to sulk alone.

In any case, sustained conversation was impossible in the belly of the Whitley.

Buz was in No. 1 plane, along with Safaryan, P.B., Deacon, a couple of pick-of-the-bunch marksmen and the squadron's number two weapons instructor, CSM Paddy Gogarty. It would be Gogarty's job to see to it that the partisans knew how to handle the motley collection of arms that were being dropped into their lucky laps: Stens, Thompsons and Lee Enfields, plus four rather antiquated Vickers MGs, four LG 40 recoilless guns, plus two 3-inch mortars and a Vickers-Armstrong anti-tank gun, chained to a sled; plus fat bolts of special plastic explosive with primers and detonators. It was the usual paraphernalia with which the SAS wreaked havoc on the Germans, friendly little weapons and all very portable. Explosives and bulkier pieces, packed in cotton wadding in wicker baskets, rode in plane No. 10, accompanied by a couple of nerveless corporals who would see to it that the stuff was shoved out over the right valley and not on to a mountain-top or into a lake.

SAS leader and second in command to Safaryan, Major Walter Oram was in plane No. 2, along with nine of the regiment's toughest warriors. In the third plane came six fighting soldiers plus the radio operators, both of whom spoke basic Russian, and special lightweight receiving and transmitting sets with batteries and charging engine. The rest of the flight was composed of a typical SAS mix of ex-infantry, gunners, engineers and commandos, seated nose-to-nose in rows of five in the Whitleys' cramped interiors, all of them, Buz was willing to bet, just as pissed off as he was at being yanked out of Libya.

The night flight was cold, cramped, monotonous and noisy. In battledress suit, snow-coloured coverall and boots, a trip to the chemical w.c. behind a canvas curtain towards the tail became a major exercise. But the crawling of men back and forth over others' knees was the only diversion throughout the long hours of the flight across Turkish airspace, that and the dispensing of flasks of luke-warm coffee and fish-paste sandwiches.

At first, apart from an occasional lurch, the passage was smooth enough and Buz eventually muttered himself to sleep, head resting forward on his arms, his arms on his knees. Beside him, P.B., who had not been born to fly, retched quietly and undemonstratively into a wad of old towels he had brought along for the purpose. Even the half-pint bottle of Scotch carried snug inside his battledress was no comfort to the corporal who, for once, could not shut an eye.

The Whitleys turned east at the corner of Mount Ararat and, to avoid flying at too great an altitude, followed the Araxes valley for a couple of hundred miles across the spur of Armenia before swinging back on line for Azerbaijan. Gradually the planes climbed towards their 14,000 feet ceiling, slanting up on charted course to clear the pale moonlit ramparts of the Caucasus.

The pilot of the first plane, Squadron Leader Watkins, had flown civil aircraft along most Far East routes in the years before the war. His navigator, Flying Officer Seale, had mustered into the RAF from a civvy job with Air Egypt. The pair had steered all sorts of gut-buckets across the inhospitable wastes of North Africa. The remaining crew members, including the radio operator, were conscripts, new to flying the large, all-metal monoplanes.

Even so, it was a fine, clear night with a silver moon, and no interception was expected from enemy aircraft or ground batteries this far from the battlefronts. Cruising speed was a comfortable 180 mph. From time to time, Watkins checked on the other planes in the formation, using the clipped, cheerful, no-nonsense jargon that only flyers really understood. The radio crackled, the Merlin engines droned loudly, the aroma of Ogden's Walnut Plug filtered back into the fuselage from the pilot's pipe.

P.B. had stopped retching.

Deacon, like Buz, drowsed in spite of the cold and the fact that the circulation in his legs had cut off several hours ago. Safaryan, however, was wide awake, purring with the thrill of being close to home again.

Forty minutes to the dropping zone.

Eighty air miles to the mouth of the valley of the Ganevis.

All was well, all was well.

The wind hit the Whitley head-on, sudden as the blow from a rifle butt.

The plane staggered.

Watkins snatched the steering as it wagged away from him. A second fierce gust followed hard on the first. The plane sawed violently. Watkins stuck his thumb in the bowl of his pipe, removed the briar from his mouth and dropped it to the floor.

'Good Lord! Where did that spring from?'

His headset crackled.

Pilots' voices spilled in upon him so loudly that he didn't even hear the querulous cries of the paratroopers behind him as they were jerked rudely out of slumber.

This was no mere squall, no transient pocket of turbulence. Though the sky ahead remained disgustingly clear, the moon untarnished by cloud, the wind had become a malicious force, a kind of poltergeist of the skies that capered with the sturdy aircraft as if they were made of balsa.

Watkins and Seale had been through this sort of thing before and were unfazed by it. Cursing laconically, they screwed up their concentration to cope with the stresses. But behind them in the string formation, less-experienced pilots fought nervously with delinquent controls as the gale tore into their planes.

46

Within minutes the formation had begun to sag and drift, two planes, the fifth and seventh, dipping towards the mountain crest below.

Quick to respond, Watkins issued orders for a replot and immediate change of course. He had received all the information he required from Seale, back in the navigator's station, and had calculated the planes' fuel reserves in relation to diversion degree, altitude and airspeed. He hoped that the wall of air that stood above the range might be no more than ten or a dozen miles thick, one of nature's aerial freaks, muck-common in mountain regions.

If he could fly around it, lead the flight to safety, he might still find the mouth of the Ganevis valley where it debouched on to the Khura-Khuva plains. Directional bearings on Baku and Tbilisi were hardly necessary. Thank the Lord he could see where he was going, plot every shiny mile, with Seale's aid, from charts and visible landmarks.

Beneath Watkins' boots, the rudder bars vibrated alarmingly.

The plane boomed with the force of the wind, drowning the noise of the engines.

In spite of his outward stoicism, Watkins began to breathe fast and shallow.

Below was the mountain called Buryakhan, summit shaped like a cardinal's hat, then, bland as a puddle of milk in icy light, the little Lake of Susanin.

The wind was to port now. There was more than just drift to contend with. The plane was being battered off course as if the gods were smiting it with iron mallets.

There was still no sign of an edge to the windstorm front. They would be out over the damned Caspian pretty soon, which was the last place Watkins wanted to be. He throttled and banked and brought her round, adjusted for severe sideslip and carved her on, slow and harsh and wallowing, towards the long horns of the mountains that flanked the Khura-Khuva, beyond which, rising high and mysterious, were the big shoulders of Sokhara and Baku-Ashran.

On Watkins' instruction, the flight endeavoured to pull itself into tight vee formation. The Merlin engines laboured. But the planes were on some kind of course again, heading for the gap in the mountain ranges. Wind velocity, the squadron leader reckoned, was three times that which would permit safe jumping. He would, of course, flutter on towards the Ganevis valley but it was patently obvious that the Russians would have to survive a while longer without the aid of the SAS.

Exactly the same thought had occurred to Buz Campbell.

Braced against the fuselage, knees drawn up, fists clutching the D-ring over his head, Buz grinned happily.

Buz had learned parachuting the hard way, by rolling backwards off trucks at Kabrit, flinging himself from jerry-built towers, diving into the sky out of a floating balloon over rough desert and from holes in the floors of Bristol Bombays. He knew enough to realize that eighty guys and a ton of equipment ejected in this sort of breeze would wind up plastered all over the map. Nope, Buz decided, the jump would be cancelled. They'd be taken home again, home to the desert and, with luck, the whole friggin' operation would be cancelled.

Cheerful at last, Buz thumped P.B.'s shoulder and held his thumb up.

Over a wad of towelling, P.B. scowled.

Unlike Buz, the little Scots corporal didn't trust anybody in this outfit to do the sane thing and, being just a wee bit cuckoo himself, didn't much care. He would prefer to fling himself down the hole rather than endure the long ride back to Syria.

Colonel Boris Safaryan was on P.B.'s side.

With thick rubber crash caps under steel helmets, ears clogged, wind howling, engines roaring, engaging in a shouting match was difficult; Deacon and Safaryan managed it, though. And Buz was quick to pick up on the fact that the sonuvabitch Russian intended to go right ahead with the jump. Gesticulating, Buz took a hand in the argument, signalling to Deacon that the friggin' colonel was off his chump and that he for one had no intention of lobbing himself into a Force Ten, not for anybody.

When the colonel crawled forward into the cockpit, pausing

by the navigator's station on the way, Buz had the sudden sickening feeling that he wasn't going to see Libya again. He was going to wind up as a mangled corpse on the side of some goddamned Russian mountain, a meal for the kites and the eagles and the wolves. Not just him: all of them.

P.B. tapped the sergeant's arm and shrugged. Across the narrow catwalk, Paddy Gogarty grinned at Buz's rage. All kinds of radio messages were humming and, against the shell of the cockpit, Buz could make out the colonel's silhouette, arm about the pilot's shoulder and, for all Buz knew, a pistol placed against the pilot's head.

When the colonel returned, he was calm: the jump was on.

Deacon made one more protest, then, not wishing to seem like a coward, accepted the decision and began setting up for the drop.

An RAF guy, complete with music-hall moustache, came back into the belly of the Whitley; the gunner/dispatcher. He opened the cover of the jump-hole and manhandled it to one side, clipping it safely to a strut. From where he sat, Buz could look down on the snows. The mountain seemed only feet below him, like he could step down on to it if only the plane would hold still for a couple of seconds. All other sounds were balled up in the papery hiss of the wind across the vent. The plane shook, shimmied, steadied. The white, white mountain slipped away from view. Craning, Buz saw the black thumb-prints of crevasses and razor-blade ridges honed sharp by moonlight.

A perfect night for a para drop – except for the gale.

The wind streamed wildly across a valley which looked like a photographic negative, black on silver.

The Whitley dove over the edge of the cliffs, lifted and swung in for the dropping run.

Like an automaton, Buz allowed himself to follow the drill. The RAF guy was grinning at him, features demonic in the glow of the signal bulb.

Back up the plane, Deacon's face was visible, handsome and expressionless as always.

Coloured bulbs winked. The dispatcher grabbed Buz's arm.

Buz straddled the hole. Below, through his knees, he could see a circlet of pale, unblemished light.

The dropping-height was three thousand feet, well below the level of the surrounding mountains. The valley here was a couple of miles wide but it narrowed fast, pinching towards the pass. The dispatcher punched Buz on the shoulder.

Buz did the little trick he had cribbed from Colonel Holms, pressed the long, felt-padded Bren bag tight against his chest so that the wallet would partially guard his face in case the slipstream snatched his body out of line on exit, protection against 'Whitley Kiss', a broken nose or split lip imparted by collision with the funnel rim.

Buz snapped his feet together and stepped forward.

Stiff and straight as a ramrod he went out of the hole.

Sure enough, the gun bag butted the funnel rim but the bag's tap on Buz's nose was light and did no damage.

Buz hadn't realized what they were into until that moment, hadn't realized how crazy Safaryan really was.

In theory the parachute would develop on static-line tug before the jumper lost much vertical height. But not tonight, baby, not tonight.

Buz was hardly clear of the slipstream which whistled along the Whitley's belly before the wind took him and hurled him away to the left.

The sergeant gasped.

He seemed to be travelling horizontally with no downward motion at all. He wriggled, waiting for the canopy, expecting to find that he had collected a thrown line or twisted rigging. Trying vainly to see what was happening behind his head, he went into an uncontrolled tumble, abruptly arrested when the chute blossomed on the end of its pay-out.

The Whitley was way over to his right now, holding a course up the valley centre. Christ! if only they had thought to drop closer to the valley's right edge. Parachutes began to open, two, three, five of them, spread out in a wild stick. Buz gulped for air, gagged. He was sheeting in on the valley wall at what seemed like the speed of light. Sweet Jesus! He dropped the gun bag on its string and felt it swing away too. What kind of wind speed was it? What kind of murder had Safaryan committed? He would kill the sonuvabitch when he got down. If he got down.

Plane No. 2 had started to crap out chutes. It was way off course, almost over Buz, drifting towards the rearing mountain wall.

The worm-cast shape of the Ganevis was far off now and Buz could see chutes opening every which way, skimming away from the flatland of the dropping-zone. His own canopy was wind-pitted, his hang far off centre and he guessed that the landing would be worse than pitching off a speeding truck on the dirt at Kabrit.

Buz struck the snow at precisely the same moment as Whitley No. 2 hit the mountain.

The sergeant didn't get to see much of the crash, only a glimpse of the dark outline of the plane, maybe a mile ahead, as it crumpled into the icy cliff. There was a splash of yellow flame and a burst of russet smoke – and that was all.

Buz came into the slope at an angle, spine bent and pelvis twisted. He tried to make a body-roll to absorb impact but found the parachute, still fat with air, hauling him like a drogue anchor. Fifteen, twenty yards he skated across rock-hard snow on his back like a beetle, legs kicking. He still couldn't get enough air into his lungs. The rigging was warped about his right forearm, nearly dragging it out of its socket. The Bren bag, scuttling along in his wake, threatened to leap on him and batter his head. He could hear the wind now, like an ocean, pounding over the ridges, scouring along the plain. A fine, freezing mist of surface snow moved in ribbons like snakes.

When the chute snagged, Buz rolled, jabbed his knees into the snow and pounced on the fuckin' thing. Slamming his arms, chest and head in to the silk, he emptied it in part with the first lunge, then crawled on to it to spill out the wind. He coaxed it in, unhitched himself and, shaking, got to his feet.

Against the mountainside, the wreckage of plane No. 2 was marked only by a smudge of smoke.

Buz sucked freezing air into his lungs.

The wind was so fierce that he could hardly stand. Across the mouth of the valley there were flames, a sparkling chain of ignited ammo; another Whitley blown into the hill? Buz scanned the sky for sight of chutes, found none at all. Whoever had got out was down. Or dead.

To his infinite relief, Buz saw eight RAF bombers clawing over the saddle of the pass, breaking away and banking.

Buz dropped to his knees. He was still shaking. He waited, watching the summits, pivoting his head this way and that, waiting for the drone and then the roar that would tell him the mad bastards had decided to come round again.

Four minutes gave to five, Buz still on his knees in the snow, still trying to breathe. And there was nothing, no sound at all except the unrelenting shriek of the wind coming in over the shoulders of Baku-Ashran. Then, startlingly, dawn broke far to the east, like a heliograph. Light seeped along the valley floor and on the high peaks the snow turned sweet and pink, like icing on a birthday cake.

Dawn.

Bang on fuckin' time.

At last Buz got to his feet, fished for the gun bag and, clutching the wallet to his breast like a rag doll, set off across the snows in search of survivors.

Deacon was still falling when the Whitley struck the mountain. In the peculiar state of near-trance which affected him every time he jumped from a plane, he witnessed the whole tragic event, including the flash-fire that swept along the plane's fuselage before the wreckage plunged into a crevasse, out of sight.

Landing, for the captain, was almost a formality, though the wind had swept him far from the river line and into the foothills to the west. When he struck the snow he was shunting at a tidy lick. He did not resist the drag of the parachute, lolling against the taut webbing with no more tension than a swimmer in a warm sea. In fact, he was preoccupied with arithmetic, with counting the chutes that dotted the dawn sky, when his canopy collapsed and bundled him into the mouth of a little gully. Quickly he clawed in the chute. Pulling it under his body, he unhitched and crawled forward to the edge of the gully, binoculars already out of their case. Anxiously he scanned the lightening landscape.

It did not occur to Deacon that the Whitleys, scared off the drop, would dare to return. Plane No. 1 was still in the sky, north over the pass, and Watkins would be more concerned with steering the crews safely back to Syria than with tacking for another stab.

Doubts jolted through Deacon's brain like electrical shocks. What shall I do if Safaryan's dead? What shall I do if the weapons weren't unloaded? How can I communicate with the partisans? Shall I be the leader, if Oram didn't get out? Would it be cowardly to abort the mission and head down the valley towards the Russian-held towns on the Caspian plains? What if I'm the only one to make it alive? Did P.B. make it? And Buz?

Deacon got to his feet and tracked the binoculars down the valley. Mountains towered over him, and in the astonishing dawn light seemed more menacing than any Alpine peak he had ever seen. For a minute or so Deacon was overwhelmed by loneliness, then, to his vast relief, saw P.B. trotting towards him over the snow slope. A Lee Enfield was slung across the corporal's back, a Thompson sub-machine-gun was in his hands, around him a rainbow aura flung up from the snow mist. The wind did not seem to bother the wee man at all.

P.B. raised the Tommy-gun aloft and waded across the gully.

'What if I'd been a German?' said Deacon.

'No bloody kraut'd be out on a mornin' like this,' P.B. answered. 'Where's Buz?'

'I've no idea.'

'I'll away an' look for him.'

'Hang on.'

'What for?'

'P.B., old man, it may not have occurred to you yet, but we're in trouble.'

'How?'

'Didn't you see the planes crash?'

'Aye, but Buz was away before us.'

'How many chutes did you count?' Deacon asked.

'Thirteen.'

'Didn't you see Buz land?'

'I was in a twist. You're the only t'come down close.'

'Don't worry, P.B. Buz'll be all right. We'll head down. Once we're on the flat, closer to the drop line, I'll fire off a few shots. It'll be daylight proper by then. I just hope to heaven there aren't any jerry patrols in the vicinity.'

'The Russian said the krauts were on the other side of the hill.'

'The Russian said a lot of things I don't really believe,' Deacon remarked. 'This operation is the most hare-brained thing I've ever heard of.'

'Big wind done for it,' said P.B., stoically. 'Wasn't the Ruskie's fault.'

'You'd go anywhere for action, wouldn't you, McNair?'

'Right,' said P.B. 'C'mon an' we'll find Buz.'

Bent into the teeth of the gale, the SAS men headed off the base of the mountain and stumbled through fluted drifts towards the river a mile below.

The Russians' fire, one of five brushwood pyres intended to pinpoint the dropping-zone if the night had been cloudy, gave off no smoke at all. Fanned by the big wind, the dry tinder glowed like a furnace and could not be missed during the five or six minutes that it took to burn out.

Catching sight of the signal, Deacon and McNair changed direction and headed down the valley towards the red glow and the group of black-garbed partisans.

On the flat, the going was easier.

P.B. complained that they should go search for Buz but Deacon drove the wee man on. He was sure that Buz would respond to the sight of the fire and come down off the mountain or across the plain. The enormous scale of the valley made it difficult to spot single figures at a distance. Reaching the river bank, Deacon found that Safaryan had been wrong; the Ganevis was not frozen solid. It flowed under thin panes of surface ice. Breaking out at falls and stony rapids, manes of spray, flicked by the gale, showered the banks and rattled on the soldiers' helmets and stung their cheeks as they followed a trail of sorts to the Russian bonfire.

Eight of the SAS detachment had reached the meeting point before them, including CSM Gogarty and Major Walter Oram. Deacon was relieved to see the senior officer.

Almost twenty years older than the captain, Oram had no business to be on such an exacting operation. But he had spent half his adult life in lands below zero and had served for twenty months in a commando unit before transferring to the SAS. He had a crumpled, seamed face, hooded eyes and a walrus moustache and, in Deacon's opinion, looked more strained and shaken than any of the others. Oram had jumped from the Whitley fifteen or twenty seconds before it drifted into the mountain wall. He was one of only three troopers to escape.

He greeted Deacon bleakly.

'Not a happy landing, Jeff.'

'No, I've seen better.'

'How many got out?'

'Probably not more than a dozen.'

'I must share the blame for this fiasco, you know. Safaryan talked with me on the plane's radio. I agreed that, having come so far, we should risk a jump.'

'Where is Safaryan?'

'He went out with the first stick. I didn't see any of you come down.'

'Look, Walter,' said Deacon, 'what are we going to do about survivors? There may be injured men up there by the wrecked planes. If not our chaps, airmen.'

'Fortunately these gentlemen have arranged to send out search parties from their villages.'

There were four Russians, elderly men who reminded Deacon of Highland ghillies. They had that same indefatigable air of self-assurance. Two wore skis, long flexible rods of polished wood clamped on to army boots. Short-muzzled MGs were slung across their shoulders and ammo belts wrapped round them like cummerbunds.

The partisans bowed and showed their teeth by way of greeting.

One said, 'We are pleased it is welcome. I am Victor. He, Vlad. Them called Peter and John. Easy, okay?'

'Very easy,' said Deacon. 'I am called Deacon.'

With uncharacteristic diplomacy, P.B. offered his whisky bottle and cigarette packet. A solemn ceremony of sipping and smoking took place between the Scot and the Russians.

The sun inched higher and the great stains of shadow on the mountainside shrank.

Three more SAS troopers trudged down from the slopes and were questioned by Oram; they had seen nobody else up there. It was now an hour and a half since the first parachute had opened, and there was no sign yet of Buz Campbell or of Colonel Safaryan.

Anxiously Deacon scanned the valley.

It would be next to impossible to string out an SAS search party. He would have to trust the Russians and hope that they found Buz and Safaryan. By Deacon's reckoning, all the men who had actually jumped were accounted for, except the colonel and the Canadian. As to those poor beggars who had been in the planes, he feared that they would not have survived the crashes.

Oram said, 'The plane carrying most of our equipment was one of the ones to crash, Jeff. The mortars and guns went with it. I've one sack of climbing gear; crampons, ropes and assorted hardware, and that's about it. God, I don't even have a gun to call my own.'

'Perhaps they'll loan you one of theirs, major,' P.B. remarked.

The Scot had been drawn to the Russian Tommy-guns like a magnet. The weapons had been made in a forge in one of the hill villages, cobbled up from damaged Russian and German arms to fit the calibre of bullets that the Caucasians had on hand. Though crude in appearance, the guns were sturdy and functional, riding on a short leather strap across the shoulders. The Russian named Vlad demonstrated, whipping the gun over his head and into a firing position with a speed that even the quick little Scot would have been pressed to equal.

'Not bad,' said Oram. 'But I think I'd prefer a British three-inch mortar, thank you.'

'Didn't the radio ops get out?' asked P.B.

'Good point,' said Deacon. 'Walter?'

Oram shook his head. 'It looks like we're cut off and on our own.'

'Look, we'll have to make a decision,' said Deacon. 'We can't hang about here. Apart from being exposed to attack, it's also damned cold.'

'Decision? Forward or back, do you mean?'

'Yes.'

'Well, I would have thought that was obvious,' said Oram. 'What would be the use in trekking back into town? It might be weeks before we could be pulled out. There is, too, the possibility that the planes might return with the rest of the detachment.'

'But not for thirty-six hours at least,' said Deacon. 'It'll take them that long to service and repair those antique Whitleys.'

Oram cleared his throat. 'Victor, where exactly *are* the Germans?'

'In Dzera, over mountain.'

'How many?'

'One corps panzers. Thirty tanks. Not good tanks for mountain road. Heavy and—' The Russian held his hands apart.

'Broad-track. Probably the new Tigers,' said Oram. 'Yes, go on. How many soldiers?'

'Panzers, three hundred. Yesterday, more. Footing. March-march. With skis.'

'Jäger,' said Deacon.

'Alpine troops.'

Victor said, 'We stop them. We go into Dzera last night. Blow up some tanks.'

'The jerries wouldn't much care for that,' said Oram.

'Make stay, for time,' said Victor. 'We know you come help.'

'There's your answer, Jeff,' said Oram. 'He's quite correct: we come help.'

'With fourteen men and practically no equipment?'

'Come, come, you help?' said Vlad, anxiously.

'Aye, sure!' P.B. patted the partisan's arm. 'We're the boys for that okay. We come help, right.'

Deacon shook his head ruefully.

Stepping away from the Russians, he went over to the troopers who were huddled by the embers of the fire trying to light a cook-tin, a task which defeated even the brew-up experts of the SAS, so strong was the wind.

'Anyone prefer to go home?'

'How far is it, captain?'

'About fourteen hundred miles.'

'What's the alternative?'

'Thirty miles to the top of the hill and a fight at the end of it.'

'Sounds like a soft option. We'll plump for the hill.'

'In that case,' said Deacon, 'I suggest we toddle.'

'Ain't we waitin' for the mad Ruskie, captain?'

'Do you feel more secure, Patterson, when the Red colonel's with us?' said Deacon.

'Feel more secure when he ain't.'

'In that case, let's go.'

Minutes later, lugging their weapons, the detachment of fourteen SAS troopers set off along the bank of the Ganevis, heading for the high pass thirty miles away.

The wind was unrelenting, though the sky was unblemished blue and the sun bright. Snow and wind, altitude and distance notwithstanding, the men of the Special Air Service expected to make five miles in every hour. When it came down to it, this was the price they paid for their status as raiders, for the joy of fighting, for the privilege of being lobbed out of a long-distance aircraft in the heart of the Caucasus; they marched like devils.

Seven miles along the valley floor, at the last of the brush-wood beacons, Deacon called a halt. Their guide, Vlad, lit the kindling and the men warmed themselves for ten minutes while flames devoured the dry wood.

The signal fire brought no response from any quarter, no gunshots, no flashing mirror, no whistle. The frozen, inhospitable landscape had swallowed up Buz and Safaryan, along with the rest of the dead.

Chance brought Buz Campbell and Boris Safaryan together. They met on a section of steep, ribbed snow which draped down from a ring of boulders at the watershed of a summer stream. The colonel was cheerful, grinning like a maniac. Buz was tempted to strangle him right there and then, bury his fat little body in the snow. He contained himself.

'We are down. Here we are, down,' Safaryan crowed. 'All one piece, sergeant?'

'Sir.'

'Good, good.'

'We lost men, sir.'

'Lost men? No, we are all down, those who jumped.'

'One stick, and stragglers.'

Safaryan did not understand the sergeant's gloom. He had seen the transporters crash, seen the rest of the flight wing away out of the dangerous mountains. But none of it counted. If he had been a German instead of a Russian, he would have backed quality against quantity any day of the week.

'No big guns, no explosive,' said Buz, sourly.

'I find you dynamite.'

'And Cordtex and primers?'

'Everything we need, here.'

In the sergeant's face, Safaryan saw a scepticism that amounted to disbelief.

'Maybe the cargo dropped,' the colonel said.

With withering patience, Buz studied the valley.

'Where, if I might inquire?' he said.

'Here, somewhere.'

Kneeling, Buz opened the Bren bag to check the weapons he had brought with him, each stoutly wrapped in an inner quilt so that the mechanical parts would not be damaged.

'Somewhere,' Buz said. 'Right.'

'My friends will find.'

Buz did not even deign to reply.

To keep from losing his temper at this fuckin' idiot, he spent some minutes on his knees, checking the guns. The Sten was okay. He wrapped it again, his back to Safaryan, and unrolled his pride and joy, a Vaughan shotgun.

Buz had bought the gun eight months ago from a shifty little agent in Cairo and carried it about with him as other mortals carried snapshots of their wives and lovers. The Vaughan seemed an inappropriate weapon for a fighting soldier but it had proved to have a hundred uses, apart from blowing the heads off Germans. Buz fingered the stock and wondered what it would do to Safaryan's brains if he just happened to stick it up the Russian's nose and pull the trigger.

'You see nothing but snow and ice. But, I tell you, many people, many fighters here,' the colonel said.

Buz got to his feet. 'I think we should be looking out for the unit, colonel, them as got down in one piece.'

'See, it is light.'

'Yeah!'

Boris Safaryan raised both arms as if to welcome the new day.

'Jesus!' murmured Buz under his breath.

The bloody colonel faced the east, arms akimbo, staring directly into the sun's diamond rays.

Buz slung the gun bag on to his shoulder. He had been informed – by Safaryan, of course – that there would be skis and food and partisans and that he wouldn't have to tote his own gear, and a lot of other shit, much of which, he had to admit, he had swallowed like a green recruit. Now he was alone with the colonel half-way up a mountain, without proper gear, with not another living soul in sight, and ninety per cent of the bloody detachment on its way back to Syria and the other ten per cent scattered far and wide. Naturally he was sceptical about this partisan army. What would it amount to, he wondered; twenty men with pitchforks?

The wind made his eyes water, and his hands, which he had

ungloved to check the weapons, were like lumps of raw meat in a butcher's freezer. He blew on them before he put on his mittens and overgloves. He listened to the howl of the wind, his back to it, and squinted again at Safaryan. The colonel was acting like a lunatic, dancing and poncing on the ribbed snow, waving his stumpy arms.

Bonkers, Buz thought; the bastard's gone completely bonkers.

And then, squinting against the sun, the Canadian saw them coming across the snow skirts, riding the fall line, a dozen of them on skis, flying fast, carbines across their backs. The members of the patrol were garbed in classy white ski-suits, hooded and booted. The ace instructors of the Middle East Ski School, on one of their challenge afternoons, never looked half so professional as that peasant brigade. Swooping, the partisans fanned out and arrived in a glittering shower of snow particles, making a circle round Buz and Safaryan.

The suits were of white kidskin leather, thonged and horn-buttoned. The goggles were tinted. The skis were Alpine. The guns weren't carbines but Mannlicher semi-automatic sniper rifles drilled and tapped to accommodate telescopic mounts. Each skier wore an identical kidney-pouch of cream leather on a plaited leather belt, and a side-arm holster. It was the most efficient mountain unit Buz had ever clapped eyes on, a far cry from ragged SAS raiders who, somehow, always contrived to look as if they had been put together by Dr Frankenstein.

The trousers were heavyweight, shaped like riding breeches into the straps of the boot tops. Boots were fur-lined. Each man there must have cost two or three hundred quid to clothe and equip. Buz's cynicism melted, his scathing opinion of Safaryan with it. If the rest of the partisan army was this good, the SAS would have their work cut out to keep up.

The unit leader, almost as tall as Buz, swaggered forward, without inhibition, took the chubby little Russian and, lifting him off his feet, kissed him on the mouth.

Throwing bach the ski hood, the unit leader shook out her hair, blonde and lustrous. She laughed throatily.

'Boris, my love. How good to have you home.'

'Jesus!' Buz exclaimed, anger wrung out of him. 'It's a bloody woman.'

'My sister, Antonina,' said the colonel proudly.

The girls of Nina Safaryan's patrol giggled at the Canadian's amazement.

'They're *all* bloody women!' Buz said.

'The most beautiful soldiers in Russia,' Safaryan declared, 'and, I tell you, the most deadly.'

The other hoods were coming down. It was like flowers blooming, the girls' beautiful faces exposed. Buz had the wonderful feeling that they were vying with each other, showing off to him. He pulled himself up to his full height and stuck out his chest, cocky now. All that pussy helped blot out the wind and the snow and made him forget the Africa Korps back home in Libya.

Few of the girls were as husky as Safaryan's sister. Most were dainty with Oriental features and a dusky tint to their skins. However much like a male combat unit they appeared from a distance, up close they were all female.

They giggled when Buz, as jovial as bloody Boris now, called out, 'Good morning, ladies.'

He scanned the circle, speculating on what treasures lay beneath the cream kidskins and which of the girls he would have first, then Antonina Safaryan clasped a hand about his arm.

'You are not English?'

'Canadian,' Buz replied.

She had a wide, generous mouth and when she smiled at him her eyes lit up with frank sexuality. Her hand tightened on Buz's forearm, the kind of welcome that Buz had never had before, in Libya or anywhere else.

'No Englishman,' she said, 'could be so handsome and so strong.'

'Well, I—' Buz fumbled for words.

'We will fight together, you and I,' the woman declared.

The fact that she came on even more gung-ho than her brother was lost on Buz Campbell. He stared into her face, into her eyes.

'Side by side,' she told him, 'we will slay many Germans.'

'Right.'

'I am strong too.'

'I can see that, Miss Safaryan.'

'Nina.'

'Buz.'

'Buz, it is a man's name. You will kill Germans with me?'

She might have been asking him to pick tulips.

Buz was oblivious to the silence around him as the younger girls watched the unsubtle seduction. Nina Safaryan was a weapon of war of a kind that Campbell had not encountered before. He was under her thrall from the first moment of meeting and would have taken on the panzers single-handed if she had asked it of him.

'As many as you want,' Buz said.

'Natalya, skis for this man,' said Nina.

Instantly a striking, beautiful girl, hardly taller than Buz's belt buckle, produced a pair of Alpines, complete with poles.

Safaryan spoke in Russian, but the woman stopped him.

'English, my love,' she said. 'We must speak English when we can or my comrade will not understand. I will have no secrets from him.'

'Of course, dearest,' Safaryan answered. 'Where are others?'

'Two parties have gone to locate the crashed aeroplanes. Vlad and Peter, with Victor and John, are at the meeting place.

'How many chutes got down?' Buz put in.

'Fourteen.'

'Christ! Is that all?'

'Before the last plane crash, it throws out chutes, not soldiers.'

Buz glanced at Boris Safaryan. 'The explosives?'

'It is right. I told you. We will find.'

Nina said, 'Ten miles, Boris, and much climbing.'

'Vlad will take the British to Roshtan?'

'It is arranged.'

'Sure, sure,' said Safaryan. 'We go to Tarek, yes?'

'They are there, yes.'

'Who?' said Buz.

It had occurred to him that P.B. would be concerned about him, Jeff too. He owed it to them to link with the unit as soon as possible. He looked again at Nina Safaryan. To hell with Deacon and McNair. And regulations. It was obvious that the Safaryans had this operation nailed up and that the spoiling effect of the big wind on the landing of troops and guns wasn't going to stop them.

'Those who are left,' said Safaryan, in answer to Buz's question. 'All who are alive of our army, trained partisans.'

'How many would that be?'

Safaryan shrugged.

'Two hundred,' said Nina.

'How many Germans?'

'Five hundred.'

Buz rubbed his gloved hand over his face, hearing the rasp of stubble. He probably looked like hell.

Five hundred razor-sharp panzers against two hundred shavetails.

The swagger was forced, the grin close to a grimace.

'My kind of odds,' Buz said.

The little pussycats were knotting up their ski-hoods, stamping the rods into the clamps again. Buz put on the skis that he had been given, made sure that they were secure. He shouldered the Bren bag and laced his fingers into the pole-loops. Boris Safaryan was clamped into a pair of Alpines too. Buz just hoped he could keep up.

The girl called Natalya swooped off across the breast of the slope, followed by a file of skiers.

For a brief, spluttering moment, common sense stirred in Buz Campbell.

'Colonel,' he shouted. 'I should go join my unit.'

'You will do so.'

'But when?'

'Tomorrow.'

'Where?'

'Baku-Ashran.'

'But—'

Nina Safaryan gave him a vigorous shove and Buz was off and running before he knew it, flying fast across the soft slope in the chain of partisans, all the little pussycats strung out before him. Nina and the Red colonel behind.

The big wind leaned heavily in his flank as the mountains that defended the narrow side valley of Tarek closed in. The Bren bag thumped against his rump and the ski-goggles pinched the bridge of his nose.

Buz had no idea of where he was headed or of what he would be expected to do when he got there.

Kill Germans? More than likely.

Side by side with the beautiful Russian girl, big and bushy as a tree? He hoped so, he surely did.

He gave a grunt, of pleasure not complaint, and dug his ski-poles into the hard-packed snow, putting the disastrous night ride temporarily out of his mind.

4 Advance to contact

P. B. McNair's experiences as a soldier of the line had been limited to a single campaign in Northern France in the first year of the war. Most of his term with the Royal Langhams, an infantry regiment of no particular distinction, had been spent retreating at a high rate of knots before the German armoured divisions. No doubt he would have been condemned to die, sooner or later, in a muddy trench or foxhole with his tin helmet tipped over his nose and a Lee Enfield clutched in his mitt, a fate allotted to many of his comrades-in-arms. But P.B. had had the good fortune to team up with Sergeant Buz Campbell and, in the course of a chaotic retreat to the beach at Dunkirk, to meet with Jeff Deacon.

Under the influence of Campbell and Deacon, P.B.'s unusual talents as a warrior were encouraged to flower and, on transfer to the SAS, to come to full and fiery bloom.

McNair was a born fighter. His years as a gangster in Glasgow had bred swiftness and guile. He had been lucky to escape arrest and conviction by the police. The army had been his bolt-hole and, rather surprisingly, he had taken to a life of order and discipline. The only fly in the ointment was the boredom of barracks and the fact that most of the training was just too easily mastered. P.B. lived for, and loved, the challenge of making war; not the theory and tactics, the manoeuvring of men and machines, but hand-to-hand combat or, even better, with an arsenal of weapons.

Months in the desert, free of the trivial regulations that governed most serving men, had seasoned P.B., added a drop of phlegm to his character and a grain of patience. For the wee man, jeep raiding was the apogée of happiness, its hardships a modest price to pay for the rip-roaring thrills of small-unit warfare.

Unlike his big Canadian buddy, though, P.B. did not consider Libya to be his personal playground and the Afrika Korps his

66

only opponent. When the Caucasian trip came up he was glad of a wee change of scene and the possibility of finding a situation which was a shade less predictable than desert raiding had become of late.

For the war, the real war, its outcome and effect on the destiny of nations, P.B. spared not one single thought.

The truth was that he wanted the fighting to go on for ever; at least until he was too old to get the drop on the krauts or was wounded out. Of course, P.B. was quite familiar with the arithmetic, the bottom line total on the bill. In the end he might be charged his life in payment for pleasure. But he had faith in his speed and agility, in his luck. Dimly he realized that he would not know the limit to his powers of survival until he reached it – by which time it would be too late.

Even so, when P.B. reached the summit of the pass and he saw the kind of defences that had been prepared, the corporal felt an ebbing of confidence.

Vlad, the Russian guide, led the SAS party at an amazing lick. It was only an hour after noon when they entered the final rock-walled corridor.

The sun stood high overhead. Icicles dripped from the frescoed rocks, and from the depths of the chasm below, where the Ganevis had its origins. The stream had thawed sufficiently to give off a tinkling echo. The last slog was up a steep gradient, a half-mile long. Underfoot conditions were better here and the snow packed down by partisans' work details.

Great brown worms of rubble, spaded from trenches, flanked the trail through a 'lane' in timber and wire tank traps. There were trip-wires all round, ready to be stretched across the surface of the snow. Even P.B. found the grandeur of Baku-Ashran dramatic.

The final lift to the summit was like a gigantic railway cutting; hard to credit that it was a natural feature and not the work of engineers. The rock walls were two or three hundred feet in height, absolutely sheer. The road, snow-banked, reduced to a mere forty yards in width. The panorama of mountains and valleys was laid out with breathtaking abruptness, the walls falling away like curtains in a theatre. One minute the party seemed to be trudging right into the sky, and the next, there was the village of Roshtan and the valley of Dzera below and a prospect of snow-shrouded peaks and forested foothills stretching away as far as the eye could see.

P.B. halted and looked back down the valley of the Ganevis, up which they had struggled. The winding course of the river invited his eyes to the distant plains and the faint smudge of smoke far, far off which marked the oilfields.

The thin, cold atmosphere made the throat dry and tight, breathing laboured. The Russians, all mountain-born, didn't seem put out by it. Stripped to the waist, eight middle-aged, muscular men, in patched cossack boots and baggy pants, were digging like mad, wielding wooden spades and huge leaf-bladed hoes. On top of the rock walls, clinging to posts and netted foxholes on the lip of the chasm, were thirty or so sentinels, muffled in greatcoats and balaclavas, all of them armed. Some toted carbines, others had the home-made Tommy-guns that Vlad called *Statchels*, a word the Russians had pinched from the Germans and which Deacon said meant Stings.

The partisans of Baku-Ashran had been digging in since the first German movement of tanks from the railhead a couple of weeks ago. There had been, Vlad said, three battles along the road to Dzera and two night raids on the panzer base in the mountain town. The Germans had intercepted a train of horses bearing guns and ammunition, coming down the Dzera river from an improvised airstrip at' Volsko, a hundred and fifty miles away. The Germans had tortured and hanged the seventeen Russians who had been with the horse train. It wasn't loss of the men but loss of the weapons that worried Vlad and his comrades; they were desperately short of firepower. They had, however, taken revenge of a sort for the executions by blowing up a portion of the panzers' fuel dump, though not, alas, enough to prevent an assault.

Oram asked about air attack.

Vlad told the major that they had seen very few German

planes, only occasional spotters, and that not a single bomb had been dropped anywhere along the road.

Vlad, Deacon and Oram moved forward again, P.B. following.

A great half-gate of bolted pine logs had been erected across the mouth of the pass. Only yards from the top of the winding track from Roshtan, the timber screen was nicely sited, taking advantage of a massive boulder to narrow the route to the width of 'two mules in harness', as the Russian put it.

'See,' said Vlad. 'Tigers.'

With considerable interest, Oram accepted the field-glasses that the Russian gave him and scanned the German encampment three miles below. Even with the naked eye, P.B. could make out uncamouflaged armour on a big ledge – a mountain pasture – just beyond the roofs of Dzera.

'Are we in range of their field artillery?' Deacon asked.

'They shoot nothings on here. On Roshtan, something.'

The rest of the SAS men had come up to the timber gate too, and stood like sightseers, gasping a little but cheerful and not in the least daunted by the sight of the force below.

P.B.'s confidence returned.

Deacon said, 'You say that there are German Alpine troops, as well as panzers?'

'It is right.' Vlad nodded. 'They march from railway. Very short time.'

'Could they flank Roshtan?'

'Flank?' Vlad did not understand.

Oram took over, gesturing with his gloved hands.

'Ah!' Vlad nodded again. 'It is could so. They climb. But we see. Put out watches.'

'Have they attempted an attack yet, at night, say?'

This time the elderly Russian shook his head.

'Sir,' said P.B., 'could I have a shuftie?'

Oram handed him the powerful Barr & Stroud binoculars. P.B. went forward and lay on his belly on the snow by the track side. Propped on his elbows and chest he trained the lenses. He made the recce thoroughly, tracing the route downward from his position, adjusting focus carefully as required.

Roshtan looked quite a squalid wee hole. He had seen better-built pigstys. Flat-roofed thatch. A boulder dyke ran round the front of the cluster of houses. Brown slush piled up everywhere. Inside the dyke were piles of wood and a couple of guys hacking away with axes. He searched in vain for anti-tank guns or other artillery. The bloody place looked near-deserted. Snow blankets on the house roofs told him there was no heat within, nobody shacked-out.

Vlad came up behind him.

P.B. squinted up at the Russian. The brown-yellow complexion and dark-brown eyes, leathery seams under the eyes and down the sides of the mouth, reminded the Scot of a notorious gangster who had terrorized the Gorbals back in Glasgow seven or eight years ago. Vlad could have been Chic's father.

P.B. stirred his forefinger. 'No wire?'

'Short wire.'

'No anti-tank guns? Boom-boom?'

'Short guns.'

'How about soldiers? Ping, ping, ping?'

'Plenty soldiers.'

'Where?'

Vlad chuckled like an old devil, the way Chic used to do before he sliced off somebody's lug with a cut-throat razor. 'No see.'

P.B. frowned and returned to the recce.

Two hard-grafting guys with axes, and not another soul in sight.

Vlad said, 'Plenty mines.'

'Where?'

'Stone wall below. Night. Dark. Put down. One hundred.'

'That's more like it.' P.B. said.

He scanned the track that wriggled from Roshtan down into Dzera.

The krauts would have no option but to come up that open road. He wondered how they would do it. Send grenadiers and infantry to take Roshtan, secure it, then make a push for the pass itself? It would be bloody murder if they did. He smiled, thinking only of himself again. Sniper's instinct. Christ, there were dozens of places he could station himself for pot-shots at the advancing krauts. He could start picking them off at about a thousand yards, though the flat trajectory against the down-hill angle would make the kind of accuracy that P.B. was used to tricky. From the back of the wall at Roshtan, though, he could shoot holes in an ace of spades. He would have no problem in taking out men as soon as they showed their snouts above the edge of the table. If the panzers came behind tanks, he would give them equal trouble, ping bullets through the tanks' apertures, force the buggers to seal up and drive blind.

P.B. was excited now. The fatigue that the hard march up from the river had engendered was washed away by the prospect of making his best bag of krauts. His total so far in one action – five hours of sniping – was one hundred and seven dead and sixty-three wounded.

He had done that job from rock cover in a Wadi where a crippled company of Afrika Korps panzers had been cut off, waterless, for four days. When the SAS raiding party – nine Willys jeeps and one platoon truck, fifty-two men in all – had run low in big ammo, Deacon had sent P.B. in with the rifle and a sack of charger clips. After five hours of jinking among the rocks, never more than seven hundred yards from the krauts, P.B.'s aim-eye began to water too badly to continue, thanks to the sand and the angle of the sun. But the krauts had had it anyway and the hundred or so still alive wagged the white flag and the SAS copped the lot, including five officers, though the tanks were pretty well clapped-out and not worth salvaging.

But his eye wouldn't water here, and the sun wouldn't bother him much since the mountains would shade out low rays.

Sighted on the base encampment, Dzera, P.B. counted all the krauts he could see. He got up to a couple of hundred before he wearied and, pushing himself upright, returned the glasses to the major and went back to unbag the rifle and put himself into the right frame of mind for a shooting spree.

All P. B. McNair now needed to be content was a hot meal, a couple of hours' shut-eye, and news that Buz Campbell was alive and well.

He didn't have to wait long.

The kid appeared in the camp at Baku-Ashran about three in the afternoon. By then P.B. had been fed luke-warm stew made from barley and mutton scraps and, like most of the SAS men, had rolled himself up in scrounged blankets and, in the lee of the pinewood gate, had fallen asleep.

When the sun slid away behind the mountains, however, the cold became intense and P.B., with the blanket around his shoulders like a cape, was wide awake when the kid skied up the pass and headed straight for Vlad.

Five minutes later, Deacon came to him.

'Buz is absolutely fine, P.B.,' the captain told him.

'Aye, I guessed he would be,' P.B. answered, hiding his relief.

'He's with Safaryan. They've gone to assemble reinforcements, local partisans.'

'We'll maybe not need them,' said P.B.

'What do you mean?'

'I could hold yon village m'self.'

'I hope you're right, P.B.,' Deacon told him. 'Because that's our job. Hold Roshtan until the Red Army gets here.'

'Red Army?'

'Red Army,' Deacon said. 'The first division is expected in about four days.'

P.B. got to his feet, the blanket slipping from his shoulders.

'How're the Russians comin'?'

'Down the highway.'

'Haud on,' said P.B. 'Those krauts down there, you mean to say they're goin' to be trapped between the pass and the Russian Army?'

'Yes.'

'An' they'll know it?'

'Without doubt.'

'So they've got no place to go, an' nothin' to lose?'

'They must take the pass or die on the Red Army's bayonets, yes.'

'Cornered rats?'

'Precisely,' said Deacon.

P.B. glanced at the sky, at deepening blue and long, purple shadows on the chasm walls. The flames of the cooking fires had become brighter and more apparent now.

'It'll be a dawn attack,' P.B. said.

'I imagine so,' said Jeff Deacon. 'Though I wouldn't be surprised if the Jäger made a sortie under cover of darkness.'

'We'd better get down there then, an' dig in.'

'That's the idea.'

'How many?'

'Us – the SAS.'

'Just fourteen men?'

'I'm afraid so.'

'Yon village can go, right?'

'Yes, it's dispensable,' Deacon replied.

'It's the pass that counts?'

'Yes.'

'An' how about the SAS?'

'Dispensable,' said Deacon.

'Better us than Russians?'

'In a nutshell.'

'Do the lads know the score?'

'Not exactly.'

'Why'd you tell me then?'

Deacon paused. P.B. had seen that innocent, eyebrow-raised expression on the young captain's face before. He knew what it presaged.

'Christ!' P.B. said. 'We're t'be first in an' last out, as usual.'

'I didn't think you'd mind,' said Deacon.

P.B. laughed drily. 'Nae bother.'

Twenty minutes later, in pairs, the SAS men slithered quietly from behind the wooden barricade and, on borrowed skis, glided swiftly down to the hill village of Roshtan, that primitive hold in the Caucasus which they were committed to defend to the death.

Extract from the War Diary of Generalmajor Erich Münke

Both Gord and I were under orders from General Brandt at Divisional Headquarters. Brandt was under orders from the Führer. By mid-afternoon on the day of the British landings, it became apparent that Brandt was in no position to supplement the Führer's promises of additional support and that our fuel loss would not be made up. Gord put in a final request for Luftwaffe support then returned to the tent to inform me that, in his opinion, we would have to act upon our own initiative and cope with Baku-Ashran's stiffened defences as best we could.

Though only eight RAF transporters has been counted, we could not be sure that ten or twenty more had not been involved in the drop, undetected by our spotters. Lack of information was the main disadvantage of being a vanguard assault. We had no real knowledge of what we were up against. The quality of arms that Gord had redeemed from the partisans indicated that the Russians were not well-equipped. It was reasonable to assume that they would feel the loss of the cache, particularly the ammunition. Even so, my initial enthusiasm had dwindled and I felt more inclined to sympathize with the Oberführer's frustration. Capturing Roshtan, let alone the pass, would be very difficult after all.

In clear weather – morning fog had not materialized, thanks to the gale – a pincer attack by the Edelweiss did not seem to be recommended. Bearing in mind the partisans' suicidal ferocity, and the fact that women and little boys fought like men, I was no longer keen to dispatch unsupported units into the forests and on to the ridges by night. Gord and I were in agreement on this score. He did not chide me, as many an SS officer would have done, for lack of determination. Gord had his own problems.

Panzergruppe 11 *were saddled with tanks that were not suitable for the terrain. The PzKpfw VI model, Tiger I, had only been in production for a matter of months. Without question, it was the most powerful tank in the world at that stage in the war. It boasted an 8.8 cm gun capable of firing 92 rounds and was protected by armour plating so thick that most frontal shots would not penetrate it. Even so, when the new Tigers had been thrown into battle near Leningrad in August of that year, they had proved less than effective, particularly on poor ground.*

The Führer believed in the Tiger, however. It was on the Führer's instructions that Panzergruppe 11 *had been furnished with thirty of them in the ill-founded premise that taking the pass at Baku-Ashran would be easy and that Tigers would come into their own on the dash to the oilfields. The Führer's assessment of the Tiger's merits was correct. But his grasp of the problems inherent in storming the pass was weak. A Tiger's range was limited. It had an overlapping suspension. The road wheels were supported by no less than sixteen torsion bars which were prone to freeze up and jam the tracks, making dawn attacks impossible. Wide tracks and heavy mantlets were unsuited to travel on such a steep, snowbound road as that which climbed to Roshtan. Gord explained all this to me in apologetic whispers, as if to keep the truth from his officers who, of course, were already fully aware of the Tigers' shortcomings. But the Oberführer had his pride and did not wish me to suppose that he was reluctant to thrust on and upward.*

I spent Thursday morning in reconnaissance and in the afternoon drilled my boys for a frontal attack on the walled village on the hill above. It was strange to be able to use the target as if it was a three-dimensional model on a board, to point my finger and explain how the arrowhead would split, how the barrage would be lifted, how the tanks would follow us in one mighty push, while Roshtan sat there, sharp and clear, only spitting distance from our muster.

In gathering dusk, I repaired to a meeting with Gord in the long tent. There, a message was brought to us that our spotters had identified as British a group of skiers who had descended from the pass to the hill village. Interestingly, no other activity, apart from a couple of men chopping firewood, had been sighted all day long. Gord's suggestion that the partisans were trying to lure us into a trap struck me as sensible. The movement of soldiers into Roshtan indicated that the partisans anticipated a frontal assault and were preparing for it.

As soon as it was dark I put twenty of my Jäger and four of Gord's observers across the bridge and let them worm their way upward for a mile or so. From that position they would be able to hear, if not see, any movement of field artillery that the British and Russian parties might attempt after nightfall. I pitied the nightwatchers. It would be intensely cold out there. But they had sleeping sacks of goose down and rubberized 'elephant's trunks' to keep out the worst of the wind, and were well-used to bitter watches. Every four hours four men returned to Dzera and reported 'No activity'. In my cot in the long tent, I managed to sleep undisturbed for almost six hours.

I was awakened at five a.m. I breakfasted with my officers and senior NCOs, a ritual I had inaugurated when a colonel, and which I saw no reason to abandon after my promotion. We ate the same food in the same conditions, cracked jokes together, reminisced about past victories and encouraged each other heartily until we were ready to go out into the freezing blackness of the morning, assemble the boys and move out to battle.

It was a quarter to six when I returned, at Gord's request, to the long tent.

'Stalin,' Gord said, without preamble, 'has ordered a battalion of the Red Army to retake the railhead at Kareva.'

'How far off are they?' I asked.

'A dawn attack is expected.'

'When did you receive this news?'

'Four a.m.,' Gord said. 'It was hoped that the Red Army

might be deflected at Algama, but their numbers proved superior and the Gruppenführer – Brandt, I mean – was obliged to order a fall-back.'

'Is it an armoured battalion?'

'Yes.'

'If they succeed in taking Kareva,' I said, 'will Division be able to mount—'

'No,' Gord cut me off. 'If Kareva falls, the Red Army will be snapping at our heels within three days.'

'Our escape route will be blocked.'

'Our only feasible escape route, Münke,' Gord said, 'is over the summit of Baku-Ashran.'

'Do you mean that we cannot pull back even for repairs and regrouping?'

'I mean just that, my friend.'

Gord wore a greatcoat with a fur-lined collar which, flipped up against the cold, framed his pallid, cadaverous face in the light of the lantern. Even younger than Gord, and impossibly thin, Schenken had no fur on his coat and wore a scarf of bright red wool. Both SS officers smoked incessantly and the air was wreathed with the fumes of their cigarettes.

I said, 'We must break out or be captured.'

'Ach, no, Münke. We will not be captured.'

'I understand your sentiments, Gord, But the Edelweiss is not a suicide squad. I will take them only as far as we dare go – in battle, I mean. I will not throw my boys' lives—'

Again Gord interrupted me. 'Münke, we are in this mess together. Are we not all Germans, good Germans?'

'Meaning?'

'Meaning, my friend,' said Gord, 'that we must win through to the Ganevis valley and drive on to Baku, or die in the attempt.'

'How many of us will finish that journey, do you suppose?'

'Enough,' said Gord. 'One hundred men and one Tiger tank will be enough. If I, or you, or Schenken here, can report that the Caucasus have been breached, that we are running free towards the oilfields, Hitler will move heaven and earth to

drum up support. Air support, land forces dropped by the Luftwaffe. Once more we will become the Führer's mailed fist. But the sleeve will no longer be empty.'

I took his meaning: the officers and men of the Waffen SS fought for approval, for the honour of their name, with rigid indifference to cost. To the Oberführer I gave no argument. We were all strung as tightly as crossbows and the news that Gord had imparted made me afraid, though – naturally – I kept my fears well hidden.

We shook hands and went our separate ways.

We would meet again in Roshtan in four or five hours – God willing.

I went out to my command car, one of three drawn up behind the ranks. My boys snapped to attention as I climbed aboard. Standing, I gave the NCOs the signal for the advance to begin.

Even as I lowered my arm, the guns spoke.

Shells burst on the mountain, reverberating in the lacquered darkness; the softening-up barrage. My hunters doubled out of the end of Dzera's cobbled street, past the forward defence positions, and scurried over the buried bridge under a canopy of artillery fire. Ghostly shapes, skis and rifles jutting up like ebony horns, they fanned out across the roadway.

Slowly my command car rolled after them, while the Kettenrads and four big gun-tracks prowled in my wake.

My usual position in mountain assaults was in the thick of it, though I had been criticized for foolhardiness. Today, however, I held back a little, not wishing to risk my neck and leave my boys at Gord's mercy.

The guns bellowed. The mountain absorbed the shocks. The ground shook. Gradually emerging out of darkness, the visor-like wall that shored the dwellings of Roshtan to the hill was seen to be already torn by the concentrated fire-power of Gord's field guns. Crouched in ranks, five yards between each man, my Jäger troops formed a great vee across the snowfield out of which the track to the top gathered itself. The snow here was packed hard, not excessively thick, and bore the lightweight advance vehicles well. The first mile from Dzera had been gained without a shot being fired at us.

Seated in the command car, I waited, smoking my pipe, though it was too cold to taste the tobacco properly, while Gord's gunners poured shells on to the roofs of Roshtan.

Each blast seemed to loosen a little more daylight from the sky, split the blue-blackness as if it was a plaster wall.

Beside me, my driver, whose name was Karl, kept his head high, though his fists were welded nervously to the steering wheel. He was very tense and, in brief periods of silence that punctuated the bombardment, I heard his stomach gurgle. Directly behind me, squatting on a padded board, my armed bodyguards, Otto and Egon, held their MP 43s at the ready. Behind Otto and Egon, in the bed of the car, my signals NCOs checked and rechecked their box of tricks, muttering to each other constantly.

Light flooded the snowfield. It came over the shoulder of Sokhara like spears of ice, then, in seconds, warmed. My boys glanced towards it, squinting, and involuntarily hugged themselves closer to the snow.

It would soon be time for us to advance again.

Karl groped for the gear-stick and tramped hard on the accelerator, making the Opel engine roar. A plume of acrid grey fumes poured from the tail-pipe. Standing, I braced myself and surveyed Roshtan in the growing light. Thumbing the Zeiss to full magnification, I saw that the hill at the base of the wall had been mined. I could discern the craters even through clouds of drifting dust. Snow had balled the gaps, and rocks, stripped by yesterday's wind, spewed outwards in brown smears like cattle dung.

Light though the barrage had been by blitzkrieg standards, Roshtan had taken a thorough pounding. For all that, there was nobody to be seen; no corpses, no darting figures, no huddled partisans deprived of shelter. It was as if we had blitzed a piece of the mountain itself, some uninhabited eyrie of twigs and pebbles.

The bombardment ceased.

79

I counted under my breath; one hundred and one, one hundred and two, one hundred and three ...

When I reached two hundred I checked my chronometer. The timing was exact.

Turning, I shouted to my signalman. He fired a red flare. The boys set off, running hard and low across the snowfield which flanked the depression of the track, heading for the edge of table ground where the snow formed a protective roof. I let them make four hundred yards, without any sign of retaliation, without any sign of life at all up there in the ruins of Roshtan, then I took the Zeiss from my eyes and tapped Karl on the shoulder. He rolled the Opel forward, its half-tracks biting deep and strong into packed snow, surging us forward.

Otto and Egon hung on, sharp-eyed, alert, upright.

The track was good, better than any of us had expected. The wind had done its work and swept it clear of loose snow. What was left was iron-hard after the sub-zero night.

My Jäger troops were below the table edge, each individual in position, guns unslung, grenade pouches open. Behind me the Kettenrads growled and the gun-tracks gave out low barking sounds which indicated that they were already running sweetly. Already we had claimed more than half the road's length between Dzera and Roshtan. Behind and below I heard the Tigers winding up their engines and, glancing round, saw the first of them claw its way into view to take position on the start line.

There was nothing to stop us – so it seemed.

Swivelling, I ordered my signalman to fire a second flare, the green one. I watched him snap the big brown mitten from his right hand and, with the pistol already loaded, stand. He looked every inch a warrior with his arm raised and the squat pistol glinting in the sun, his face smooth, unbearded and innocent.

At the end of its long, lethal flight, the rifle bullet flew into my young signalman's chest and ripped through his lungs. Upraised arm still aloft, he fell backwards, fist snapping shut

*in rigor. The flare whizzed backwards in a corkscrew parabola
and burst into the snow among the Kettenrads fifty yards
away, spreading fire like the fronds of a sickly, green fern.*

*My signalman toppled over the gate of the command car
and the Opel lurched as poor Karl, my driver, became the
sniper's second victim.*

*I experienced no horror at the sudden deaths, only wonder
at the accuracy of the shooting. Hunched behind the car's
splinter shield, I groped for the emergency brake, Karl lolling
dead across the steering, and jerked it, shouting for Otto or
Egon to find a fresh green flare and get it away quickly. But
Otto and Egon did not respond. They were dead too.*

The second signalman was pressed flat on the boards.

*I shouted at him, 'Give me your pistol, the flare gun. Throw
it to me, lad. Come on, be quick.'*

The boy had enough wit left to do as I asked.

*I caught the heavy gun in both hands, dropped on to
all-fours, kicked open the car's offside door and dropped,
dog-like, to the snow. Rifle bullets spanged about me, scoring
the plating and facing of the shield. Defended by the car body,
I kneeled, set the flare's arc and fired the pistol.*

*The green rocket soared up towards Roshtan and burst into
a splash of colour for all to see.*

*Yelling, my hunters swarmed over the table's edge and, like
pigeons in a shooting gallery, were picked off one by one
before they made fifty yards.*

*Impotent and cursing, pinned down beside the Opel, I had
to watch the pride of the Edelweiss being slaughtered by
hidden muskets. With savage regret in my breast, rage too, I
crawled round to the back of the Opel and found the box of
flares and, on my knees like some decrepit monk, fired the
bright yellow rocket that told my brave troopers to retreat.*

*The sniper fire was unrelenting and unnaturally accurate at
the range. Eleven or twelve more Jäger were lost as they tried
to scuttle back to the table's edge, their bodies lying like ink
blots on the snow.*

It took three Kettenrads, and cost five lives, to pull me out

from under the Opel and get me back to safety by the bridge.
    *By that time I had caught Gord's disease and was burning
with a fever of revenge.*
    *I wanted those damned British snipers, wanted to see them
dead. Shot, stabbed or hanged, it no longer mattered, provided
the lives of my brave Jäger were paid for in full.*

Buz Campbell was so relaxed, so comfortable that he felt as if
he was floating in warm milk. Fine wool blankets caressed his
skin and beneath him the hay was as soft as a feather bed.

For a while he did not stir. Revelling in the sensual pleasures
of being warm again, he listened to the sounds of the girls and
smelled the musky perfume of their bodies in the stout stone hut.

Here, so Nina had told him, Caucasian shepherds lived when
their flocks grazed the high summer pastures. Here, shearing
was carried out and, if the spring was kind, late lambing. It
was a simple, snug, stone shack with timber posts, an earthen
floor and an open fireplace in which cords and little round
coalcakes were burned. It was also the headquarters of Nina
Safaryan's special ski-patrol.

All the girls, Buz had learned, were athletes, graduates of
the Georgian State Gymnasium. Many had travelled abroad
in the years prior to the war. With the blessing of the Soviet
Cultural Exchange, Nina had spent four years in France and
Switzerland learning advanced techniques of skiing and the fine
points of the rules governing international competition. As the
sister of a Red Army Colonel of Sport, and the daughter of a
Master of Sport, Nina had enjoyed many privileges, all of
which, like her brother Boris, she had exploited to the full.

Founding a special guerrilla group had been Nina's idea.
Backed by Boris, it was financed from a mysterious fund
operated through the Gymnasium by yet another Safaryan.
This uncle, Buz gathered, was quartermaster and arms dealer
for all Caucasian partisans. It occurred to Buz that the Gymnasium fund had had a revolutionary purpose of which Joe
Stalin would emphatically disapprove. But the German attack
on Russia put paid to any plans the Safaryans may have nursed

about attacking the Stalinist state from within. They would not embrace Facism as an answer to their problems or desert Russia in time of desperate need.

The Dzera partisans were far better organized than most other guerrilla groups and had wreaked havoc on the 1st Panzer Army and other units of von Kleist's Army Group A. Steppe fighting in the Don corridor, however, had reached new levels of violence. Torrents of tanks and continual bombardments checked every German thrust, as the panzers sought to wear down the roving Russian hordes. Grand strategies no longer interested Colonel Boris Safaryan. He had outthought and out-planned the pedestrian minds of Moscow's State Security and Central Staff offices. Out of a thousand possible areas of tactical conflict, Safaryan had selected the fight for Baku-Ashran as the one to which he would commit his private army. What the generals did about it was their business. Self-sufficiency was the Roshtan Group's principal weapon. With Uncle Safaryan doing business on the international market months before Hitler invaded Poland, supply chains were well established. Loyalty to Safaryan, rather than Soviet idealism, had cleansed the ranks of Dzera's partisans of collaborators and Nazi spies. Buz did not press for details of how this had been done.

If Buz has expected sober, lumpy peasants to be his comrades-in-arms, he was pleasantly surprised. Nina Safaryan's team were light-hearted, chatty and as full of zeal as bloody Boris himself. Several spoke passable English. Others tried French on the burly Canadian and all treated him as some kind of hero. Safaryan did not have to explain what was going on that Thursday and why Buz was being whipped around the villages that pegged the mountains on the sides of the Ganevis. Buz was Safaryan's token Britisher, symbol of a promise fulfilled.

Boris and Nina were powerful figures in this region but he, Sergeant Buz Campbell, was the clincher, the come-you-all, the brand of fire, harbinger of big battles and prophetic embodi-ment of victory. The hell he was! A dozen bloody SAS men with rifles and Stens?

Thursday wore on. Buz tired. His cynicism welled to the

surface and only pride, and Nina Safaryan's encouragement, kept him smiling, kept him going, until at last, around four in the afternoon, he was steered into a spur valley and up to the sheep shack to rest.

Even a heavy meal of mutton stew and tinned potato, washed down with vodka, did not rouse Buz enough to be seriously interested in Nina's offer of a companion for the night. All he wanted was a place to lie down – alone. He rolled gladly into the swaddle of blankets and was asleep almost before his head hit the hay.

It was daylight when Buz wakened.

He reckoned he had slept for fourteen hours. He was certainly refreshed enough to be roused by the chatter of all that pussy. This kind of intimacy shocked Buz a little.

The interior of the hut had the informality of an all-male barracks but none of the zoo smells. Half-naked girls moved unabashed around the trestle table preparing food while others, dressed only in knickers, came and went through the open door. Towels were wrapped about their heads and they laughed happily as if in a Bond Street salon. Buz, who had slept in his undershorts, held a blanket modestly to his chest and groped for his shirt which hung from a nail on the stall post; then he stopped reaching and stared at the rectangle of sunlight.

Framed in the doorway, Nina Safaryan beckoned to him. Each golden hair on her body was erect in the cold air. She looked, Buz thought, like a cougar. He climbed out of the blankets just as he was, leaving his uniform on the nail.

He had nothing to be ashamed of.

Nina had a towel slung over her shoulder. She wore a skimpy pair of silk pants that hid few of her secrets. She looked as if she was on her way to a hot, sandy beach instead of ready to step into sub-zero temperatures on a carpet of frozen snow.

'Come, come with me, Buz,' she said.

Challenged, Buz grabbed a towel from his kit and followed the blonde outside.

The cold was so severe that after sixty seconds you hardly noticed it at all. He saw what they were at, the girls. A deep, wooden feed-trough had been filled with fresh, clean snow and the goddamned girls were bathing in it, rubbing handfuls of the stuff all over themselves. He had heard of such regimes of hardiness, of course, and equated them with some of the crazy training schemes the SAS evolved to keep their soldiers honed and hard. But the sight of five girls massaging snow into their bare breasts and down their glowing thighs was almost too much for Buz. There was no wind, thank God. Even so, the air shrivelled his balls inside his undershorts as he pranced towards the trough, whooping as if it was some wonderful experience.

Scooping up handfuls of cold snow, he plastered them against his hairy chest; he thought his heart would seize up like a tank engine. Then Nina Safaryan's hands were on him, fistfuls of snow massaged into his back and across his shoulders. He scooped up more snow from the trough and turned on her, showering her with it, though he didn't dare put his hands on her body, on the big, bare, bobbing breasts. His skin glowed. Behind him, girls giggled and chattered like sparrows at a bird bath.

'Good!' the blonde shouted. 'It is so good.'

'Yeah!' Buz answered.

'But not stay long.'

'Right.'

'Dry now.'

'Okay.'

Turning, he braced his arms upon the trough and let her chafe him with the rough, army-issue towel. His body was suffused with blood. He could feel the old red vino pumping through him as Nina scrubbed him dry. Then, to the sergeant's surprise, she turned away from him and took position, exactly as he had done, indicating that he must return the favour.

The muscles across her back stood out, supple and strong. The curvature of her spinal column was superb, sculptured into swelling buttocks that showed just above the band of the pants. Her breasts swung as he worked on her, keeping it rough, not risking a softer touch in case he overstepped the mark of decency, wherever it was drawn.

They were like gladiators going through some ritual of cleansing, anointing themselves for mortal combat. He saw how it was with these gay Russian girls, how they kept the oppression of war and death at bay by this sort of discipline. When this operation was over and the krauts had been beaten off, he wondered if they would indulge in other disciplines, in pleasures of the flesh, if he would be part of that celebration too.

For a moment Buz was warmer than he had ever been, more alive, then the cold stung him, a breath of wind from the valley mouth which carried faint sounds with it.

Leaving the towel draped about Nina's shoulders, Buz straightened, stiffened.

'What's that?' he murmured.

The woman straightened too, hands stirring the towel across her breasts, head cocked, her hair draped across her cheek.

She knew, Buz noticed, just which way to turn.

'What the hell is it?' he demanded.

'Roshtan,' she said. 'We must go inside. We will freeze.'

'Guns,' said Buz. 'Medium stuff, but lots of them. Krauts, fuckin' krauts.'

'It is the wind, you hear the guns on the wind now,' she said.

'Is that my outfit? Are they fighting?'

'It is a barrage, against Roshtan.'

'How far?'

'Eight miles, nine.'

'That's it,' Buz declared. 'If my lot's on the line, I gotta be there with them.'

'With us, you are with us.'

'Not any more, lady.'

Buz ran back to the shepherds' hut to fling on his battledress and find his skis. If there had been no engagement, no combat, he wouldn't have given a toss for the regiment or spared a thought for the Deke or P.B. or Oram or any of them. But he couldn't swan around with the pussycats when the krauts were trying to kill his comrades. It wasn't, as Deacon would put it, cricket. He was buttoning his shirt when the woman, accompanied by her brother, got to him.

On the table were pans of lumpy oatmeal spread with butter and honey. Pots of coffee steamed by the side of the fire, real coffee, rich and fragrant. The chicks were dressed and eating, their hair soft, their cheeks glowing. Shit, Buz thought, they ain't gladiators, just kids in over their pretty heads. I got no business to be here.

Boris Safaryan said, 'Guilt, you are guilt.'

'Goddamn right.'

'No need guilt, Buz. We all go fight.'

'How soon?'

'One hour.'

'In one hour my guys could be spit-roasted by those panzer shells.'

Nina shook her head. She had put on an army shirt and ski-pants. Buz had the notion that maybe the whole idea was to keep him from fighting, some kind of soft con to sap the strength of the detachment. He had been on Russian soil for twenty-six hours now and he hadn't seen a kraut, hadn't even had word of how many of the SAS had gotten down safe. His guilt increased.

Nina said, 'All day. It will take all day, Buz, for the panzers to overrun Roshtan.'

'Yeah?' the sergeant snapped. 'How the hell would you know?'

'We are in touch,' the woman said. 'We wait for guns, then we go at once. You come with us. Second rank, yes?'

Buz hesitated. He seated himself on the blankets and reached for his ski-boots, then a sudden panic swept him and he scrabbled amid the blankets of the bed-place. He found the Bren bag and whipped it open. The Sten and the Vaughan were still there, untouched. Slightly ashamed, he glanced up at the Safaryans.

'Second rank of the attack?' he asked.

'We are those who must defend Baku-Ashran.'

Buz recalled the model that Safaryan had set up on the table of the nissen hut in the briefing room, coloured lumps of papier mâché, sponge and matchboxes. The whirlwind tour yesterday had robbed him of his sense of direction. In Libya he had a compass in his brain and could sense by instinct, like a goddamned homing pigeon, where Kabrit lay. But here in the alien mountains he was at the mercy of these Russian weirdos.

'Roshtan,' said Buz. 'The krauts are attacking the hill village below the pass, right? From their base at Dzera, right?'

'They will be stopped,' said Boris Safaryan. 'It will cost much lives.'

'Whose lives, colonel?'

'Most German.'

'Are my guys defending Roshtan?'

It had gone quiet in the hut now. The girls had ceased eating and were gathered, sheepishly, about the table or the fireplace, trying to appear unconcerned.

'Jesus!' said Buz. 'My guys *are* in the firing line, ain't they?'

'Yes, it is the SAS, Buz,' Nina said. 'The German attack began one hour ago. Roshtan will not fall before afternoon. The Germans have trouble with tanks.'

'You don't need me,' said Buz.

Buz tried not to look into Nina's eyes, illogically afraid that she would hypnotize him into compliance.

'We need to keep one back,' she said.

'One what?'

'One soldier.'

'Why pick on me?'

'Because you were there.'

'Is that the only reason?'

'You work the guns,' she said bluntly; it was a statement as positive as any Buz had heard. 'We collect the weapons dropped and scattered. You show how to work them.'

'And the special explosive,' said Safaryan.

'Did that pannier turn up?'

'It has been located,' said the colonel. 'The Vickers is on way to Baku-Ashran, very this moment. We go join to my army in one hour.'

'Then what?'

'March to Baku-Ashran.'

'How big is your army?'

'Big enough to hold the pass,' Nina answered.

Buz nodded. He was not much appeased but he saw the sense in holding a guerrilla, like himself, in reserve, to handle the British weapons that Safaryan's scavengers had found. He was beginning to understand how the Caucasian partisans operated. Much the same way as the folks back in Canada would do if an enemy rolled armour to their backyard fence, into the Rockies. Mustering a civilian army was never easy and took time. His role was really that of token soldier, a kind of totem. More important, he knew about the guns and the explosive, how to use them to best effect. Maybe Safaryan had gotten a body count, found out that Gogarty was dead. Whatever, Colonel Boris was taking no chances. Colonel Boris was setting up the last ditch defence before the first ditch had fallen.

The woman touched the sergeant's face with her fingertips. Her hands were soft against his stubble beard. Buz resisted the inclination to pull away. He didn't want to be sweet-talked, to have his thinking addled. He finished dressing, saying nothing, went to the breakfast table and took himself a bowl of the oatmeal. Still standing, he ate it hurriedly and washed it down with coffee. The girls, he noticed, moved back from him and gave him room. Boris and Nina, uncertain, murmured together in Russian, making up another plan, maybe, in case he should strike out for the pass on his own. He let them sweat it out while he finished his coffee and went outside, lighting a cigarette.

Buz stared over the mountain tops, big and clean, rinsed by night frost and the morning sun. The wind, strengthening, carried the shudder of the guns from his right, from the north-west, he figured. He looked down the spur to the wall of mountains that flanked the river valley.

Nina came to him. She was dressed in a ski suit, booted, goggles on her forehead, one of the fancy rifles over her shoulder. She waited a step or two behind the sergeant and off to one side.

Without turning, Buz said, 'How long do we have to hold this pass?'

'Three days, perhaps four.'

'Tell me the truth, kid.'

'I do not lie.'

Buz faced her. 'What do you really want from me?'

Unsmiling, the woman said, 'Your life, if necessary.'

'All right. You got it,' Buz Campbell promised. 'If necessary.'

Deacon was aware that it wasn't the tanks that were doing the damage to the stronghold of Roshtan, but the concentrated fire-power of the German field guns.

The effective range of the battle tanks' 8.8 cm guns would be about five hundred yards and the rain of shells that fell on the dyke below the hill village was far too well-patterned to come from the armoured vehicles. He had asked Vlad exactly what the Germans had down there but Vlad pretended not to understand the question, an evasion which suggested that in this instance the Russians had been less than thorough in gathering intelligence.

Gogarty's informed opinion, which Deacon was willing to trust, was that the barrage stemmed from six strategically positioned PAK 39s, captured Soviet 76 mms that the krauts had converted to their own use.

After the first ten or fifteen minutes, however, the matter of what was being fired and what was firing it became, for the SAS detachment, quite academic. Raising sights from the curve of the dyke, the field pieces found range on the buildings, and Deacon, with the others, was obliged to dive for cover in positions that the partisans had thoughtfully prepared.

The noise alone was enough to confuse the senses, and for a while retaliatory fire from the SAS men was, to say the least of it, sporadic. Only P.B., who had immediately selected a prime position, seemed oblivious to the ear-splitting explosions and the crump of solid debris around him. Sensibly, the Scot had scampered to the far right wing of the village, where the houses smeared out on to a sheep track and there were no distinguishing features to attract the gunners' attention. Here P.B. found a ready-made foxhole, a big old water-tank half buried in a snow-drift, with a runnerless sled, ten feet long and built of seasoned hardwood, to block flak.

Deacon did not underrate the courage and skill of the men at his command, or Walter Oram's ability to deploy them to best effect. Nevertheless, he was conscious of the fact that the defence had become, circumstantially, rather a paste-and-paper job and that the partisans perhaps expected too much of them. He constantly had to remind himself that it was the holding of the pass that mattered, not Roshtan, not the body count, and not the unfortunate handful of British troops who had been dumped there.

Though he had slept well, bedded in hay in a manger in a cellar stall, Deacon had no heart for a dawn fight. As Buz had done, he sensed that the weaving column of Tigers, the Jäger corps and the whining shells of PAK 39s really were props from a war he was not equipped to win. Hit and run tactics, a piratical approach, had become ingrained in Deacon too. Crouched behind mounds of rubble and slush, waiting for the panzers to come to him, he felt hideously vulnerable.

Major Oram had organized the Bren positions. Four SAS men had been blown away in the first minutes of shelling, all of them dead. With the weapons that the Whitleys had carried, weapons that were now back in store in Libya or strewn across the mountainside, fourteen Britishers might have held off the phalanx of German armour for long enough. But Roshtan, compressed into a natural bowl, was a tight target. Overrunning the village would be easy for the massive battle tanks, once they reached the broken dyke. To Deacon's way of thinking, the detachment's only hope of preventing a swift German victory was to delay the infantry for as long as possible by inflicting heavy casualties.

Yardages were important, the relative range of weapons. The SAS suffered from a dearth of armour-piercing weapons and would receive no covering barrage from the Russians. Not even the advantages of terrain could outweigh that handicap for very long.

When the barrage stopped and the white-clad German

mountain troops stormed over the edge of the ridge below, Deacon rose from his position among the rubble and headed for a vantage point on the slope to the right.

Pitching on to his stomach, he clasped the binoculars to his eyes and, with satisfaction, watched the Jäger troops twist and squirm, dropping like flies under the crossfire of the SAS marksmen. He wasn't much cop with a rifle in the accuracy stakes and, if this phase was prolonged, would act as a powder monkey, dragging ammo to the various sniper posts and taking check on the wounded.

Deacon was thoroughly imbued with the spirit of the Special Air Service, a freelance, freebooting regiment that had no truck with conceit and scorned the gulf between officers and enlisted men. Through the glasses he observed the flight of the yellow flare and, with a little cheer, saw the ranks of the Jäger slither and begin to retreat, saw the bastards flail and fall and lie still, victims of ill-planning, fine weather and brilliant shooting. A thousand yards; the thin atmosphere would add to effective range. The stammering of the Brens was the only sound around him, made innocuous by the vastness of the snow-filled amphitheatre.

Propped on his elbow, he looked over his shoulder.

The houses of the village had lost all shape. The bloody place resembled an archaeological site, all stones and pits and broken mounds of rubble. Far up, by the rectangle of the timber gate at the mouth of the pass, he could make out the partisans, quite a bunch of them, spectating anxiously.

Gogarty and Oram were of the opinion that the Germans were short of ammunition, a result of the general supply problem. Even so, if he had been the jerry commander, he would have hauled off the infantry post-haste and lashed in another couple of tons of shells. Surely it was obvious even to Waffen-SS butcher boys that Roshtan would not fall to a frontal assault conducted by foot-soldiers, not unless they had a whole division of the poor devils massed in Dzera, ready to push into the fray.

Deacon glanced at his watch: the SAS team had held Roshtan for eleven minutes.

All they had to do was multiply that by, let's see, about six hundred, and the German thrust would fizzle out and the Red Army would come whistling down the high-road from Kareva, assuming that Vlad and his chums had got the message correct and that the military did manage to capture the railhead and that somebody in authority realized there was a battle going on at Baku-Ashran and issued the order to turn east, please.

Kettenrads crept up to the halt line. It all looked deliciously chaotic down there, half-track motor bikes buzzing forth then back, gun-trucks stopped dead, the Tigers, only eight in view so far, halted, jerries crawling about like smoke-stunned insects.

Deacon lit a cigarette.

There was little point in speculating what the Germans would decide to do. He would find out soon enough. It would not entirely surprise him if there was a lull, another of those tense, uncertain pauses while generals argued with colonels and colonels argued with majors and everybody did their sums.

He peeped over the edge of the mound and, rowing himself on hands and knees, peered down the slag-slope that had, until recently, been rather a decent piece of rustic architecture, the village dyke.

A dead raven, jet-black and tidy, lay yards away. There were all sorts of subtle movements among the stones; rats and mice, of course. One unexploded landmine, like an unearthed pie-dish, was perfectly balanced on a knob of snow, its pressure prongs sticking up like metallic whiskers. The minefield had been something of a joke, a mixed protective field that had hardly had more than nuisance value. Again, scarcity of supplies had prevented the partisans doing a thorough job. The high pass was probably better defended.

The Brens and rifles had quieted.

Deacon scrutinized the line of foxholes and Bren stands. The Russian woodchoppers had done a fair job with timber and shoring. Even so, Oram was shuffling the positions, seeking more adequate cover and changes in angle of fire. Severn, Peters, Owens, McIndoe and Hargrove were all on the move. Squatting, Walter directed them like a midget traffic policeman.

Below, nothing much was happening. Medicos hadn't been sent out yet to retrieve the dead and dying from that superb snowfield, that gleaming white deathtrap. God, with mortars and anti-tank guns, what devastation they could have wreaked on the Germans. Deacon could quite understand why von Kleist's thrusts into the Caucasus had failed to penetrate the mountain wall.

P.B.'s piercing whistle attracted Deacon's attention.

The wee man was waving from the iron foxhole he had found. Deacon trotted over, head ducked below the level of the remains of the dyke.

'Got any spare fags?' P.B. asked.

Deacon extracted four Capstan from his silver case and handed them to P.B. who stowed three of the cigarettes carefully in his battered tobacco tin, and stuck the fourth into his mouth.

'Goin' t'be a big day,' said P.B. conversationally.

Deacon felt that the hunting instinct was a shade too well developed in the little Scots corporal, but he kept his opinion to himself.

'What's your bag so far?' he asked.

'Twenty-nine sure hits.'

'Absolutely tremendous,' said Deacon.

'Aye, no' bad for ten minutes on the trigger.'

P.B. flicked a match-head against his thumbnail – a trick that Deacon had never been able to master – and held the flame steady to the cigarette tip. He inhaled and lolled back against a bolster of snow by the side of the rusty water tank.

'Wonder when Buz'll get here,' said the corporal. 'Christ, he's missin' all the fun.'

'I expect there will be plenty of fun left for Buz.'

'What d'you think the krauts'll do?'

'If they have any sense,' said Deacon, 'they won't come at us head on.'

'Ach, krauts have nae sense,' said P.B.

The Lee Enfield was laid carefully on the Bren bag, reloaded and with a dozen spare clips set out in a crescent pattern ready to hand. P.B. had put on a pair of thick woollen gloves to keep his fingers warm and supple. He smoked the Capstan delicately between finger and thumb.

The sun had breached the mountain behind them now and the air was warming. The snow below had lost its raspberry hue, had turned to vanilla.

It was now twenty minutes since the Germans had sent up the yellow flare that had aborted the morning's first assault. Since then they had done nothing. They were still scattered on the snow-covered sward above the bridge, still only eight Tigers visible. Still no Red Cross or MC nurses had ventured out. Fine, thought Deacon: let them take all the time they want to, all damned day if they wish. Every minute's delay suits us.

'How many krauts did Stan knock down?' said P.B.

'Stan?'

'Vennables.'

'Oh! Unfortunately, P.B., Vennables didn't make it.'

'Bloody hell! Shell?'

'Straight into the emplacement; Vennables, Murphy, Woolton and Patterson all bought it.'

'Phil an' all. Bloody bleedin' hell!'

'They'd just finished a brew-up. They didn't have a chance to spread out when the shelling started.'

P.B. frowned but gave no other sign of being affected by the death of the four rankers, two of whom had served with the SAS since its inception.

Dying was like that, Deacon thought; not, as a rule, dramatic. One simply put down the tea can, heard the whistle of the shell, and died; or, in the midst of a perfectly fine little action, much less desperate than a dozen others that one had engaged in, suddenly there was a bullet in one's head or heart and that was an end of it.

In spite of the elaborate and fatalistic superstitions that the regiment, officers as well as men, created, demise was as random as survival. McNair might delude himself that speed and cunning gave him the favour of the odds but this was not so. The bravest and best soldiers died just as often and just as unexpectedly as incompetents and cowards – not that there were any of the latter skulking in the SAS. But it was fact, a plain and incontrovertible fact, that in war, even in training, one could be snuffed out without warning and without reason.

Deacon had lived without illusions for months now. He wondered if it was the same with P.B. He did not dare pry, however, and would have embarrassed his friend by deigning to put such a highly personal question. P.B.'s talisman, apart from the Lee Enfield rifle, was the bottle of whisky, *usquebaugh*, the Gaels' famed Water of Life, that he inevitably managed to tote about with him. Deacon had the oddest feeling that P.B. would not be killed while there was a drop left in that bottle. He would simply refuse to go.

'Did you know them well?' said Deacon.

'Who?' said P. B. McNair.

The period of conversation was brought to a sudden conclusion.

'The major wants you,' said P.B.

Oram was signalling to Deacon, shouting, 'Jeff, here they come again. Jeff, look below.'

Oram's cry was blotted out by the first screaming shell from the PAKs and he dipped out of sight, bobbing down as if tugged by a string around his knees.

For a split second the streets of Roshian, if one could call them that, were passive, then violent eruptions and great sprouts of stony earth heralded a second German advance. Debris pocked the snow around the foxhole and P.B. yanked Deacon into the water tank with him and pulled the end of the sled across the opening. Side by side, captain and corporal lay, heads down, while the brutal barrage continued. It was concentrated and fierce but did not last long, just long enough for the German commanders to swing the rest of their armour across the invisible bridge and out of Dzera on to the climbing track.

By the time Deacon scooped out a viewing slot in the snow bank and trained the binoculars, the Tigers were manoeuvring into position, a great python of them, nosing upwards in pairs.

It was hardly according to the panzer handbook but there was a desperate kind of sense in it. When the temperature rose

96

ten or twelve degrees, as it probably would around noon, the snow would lose its firmness and the progress would be doubly hard for the wide-tracked tanks. The terrain was totally unsuited to the use of battle tanks, which were most effective on a broad front and not crawling up a narrow mountain highway, but the plating and the 8.8 cm guns would make them deadly once they got within range.

Deacon studied the Tigers with interest. He had heard of Hitler's new supertank but none had so far appeared in the desert war and this was his first close-up of the beast. Whatever their shortcomings, PzKpfw VIs were obviously more than a match for rifles and MGs. Deacon doubted if anything less than a six-pounder would make much impression on them, except at very short range. Whoever was running the show, probably an SS colonel or major-general, had figured the odds very accurately and, by doing all the wrong things, had struck exactly the right approach for the situation.

Provided there were no engine failures to delay them, the column of tanks would weave slowly upwards and fan out across the easier slope only three hundred yards below what remained of the Roshtan dyke. Foot-soldiers, panzer grenadiers and Jäger troops, well protected by the armoured column, would be able to mount a sustained attack from behind the tanks. Only heavy artillery would be capable of inflicting damage on the German armour, and the Russians had nothing of any weight that Deacon had seen. Even their mortars and handful of scrappy field-pieces were dug in and mounted to protect the pass, the field of fire restricted by the shoulders of the mountain peaks.

'Christ Almighty!' said P.B. 'I canny take those buggers out with a rifle.'

'Can't you shoot through the visors?'

'Give's the glasses.'

For almost a minute P.B. McNair studied the tanks through Deacon's binoculars. The cigarette, a burned stub, clinging to his nether lip, he shook his head.

'Fuckin' slope shields,' he muttered, handing the glasses back to Deacon. 'Only a lucky shot would get past thon. The gun hangs over the aperture an' all.'

'Well, we can't just sit here and watch them. Once they get within range, in half an hour or so, we're sunk, old chap.'

'Hand-to-hand?' P.B. suggested. 'Lie low an' take them on the bayonets?'

'We'll have been pounded out of existence by then,' said Deacon. 'Even if a handful of us did survive, which is dubious, we could never hope to hold against an assault wave of several hundred armed grenadiers. Somehow we've got to slow them down, stop them before they get over the table.'

'Aye, but how?'

'Damned if I know,' said Deacon.

Walter Oram and Paddy Gogarty were crouched in the cellar of a ruined dwelling. The floor of packed earth, like most of Roshtan, angled steeply towards the valley. Sheep had been wintered in the chamber and pellets of dried dung were everywhere. With each explosion a rain of frozen dust sifted into the cellar and the sheep pellets danced like jumping beans. Neither the major nor the CSM seemed at all concerned that they were under heavy fire.

Paddy Gogarty had been foraging. A variety of useful items were spread out, like treasure, on a woollen blanket. On another blanket lay the dismantled parts of an anti-tank mine. The mine had been manufactured in the Klin Armaments Works and bore an impress mark that Oram identified as meaning 'Reject', a typical sample of the unreliable weapons that were supplied to partisan armies. Gogarty had taken the mine apart, using only pliers, an electrical screwdriver and his teeth. Design and construction were of the simplest; a pie-dish filled with 12 lb of TNT.

'What do you think, Paddy?'

Gogarty shrugged. 'For starters, the retainer springs are rubbish. Too thin and rusted to the bottom of the arming plate. Supposed to be set off by about two-fifty pounds of pressure. You couldn't set this 'un off if you ran the Royal Scot across it.'

'But is the TNT fresh?'

'Fresh as a Kerry breeze, sir.'

'Can you rig it for delayed detonation?'

'Shouldn't be too hard, provided the Ruskies have a few bits of slow fuse on the premises. What's the idea, major? The Germans aren't goin' to be sittin' still.'

Major Oram chuckled and the unlit pipe in his mouth waggled. 'Laying a mine-field at this stage in the proceedings would be a waste of effort.'

'Sure an' it would.'

'But if we had, let's say, a dozen slow-fuse minutes in good order, we could place them directly under the big tanks, just when and where we wanted them.'

'Like we done with the planes at El Dahoud?'

'Similarly, similarly.'

'But that was a raid, major. At El Dahoud the planes were static and it was night-time.'

'Have you had a look at the track, Paddy? So far it's taken little or no heavy traffic.'

'The Ruskies don't have no heavy traffic. What they got, they brought up the other side of the pass.'

'Fresh, young, untrammelled winter snow.' Oram took the pipe from his mouth and scratched the tip of his nose with it as the cellar shook with the blast of a German shell. 'Snow that has been down for a mere four weeks has certain interesting qualities, Paddy. It will – in pockets – have attained a drift depth of fourteen or fifteen feet. Tanks, of course, will crush it down and thus provide sufficient traction for a one-in-twelve gradient, which is about all the panzers will have to contend along the Baku-Ashran high-road. As we have observed, however, the high-road narrows, a half-mile up, and the panzers will be obliged to advance one tank at a time, following a restricted path around the corner.'

'But, major, maybe they'll whip the ground first.'

'Perhaps not. If they do it will only be to explode pressure mines, which is, quite naturally, what they will expect to find.'

'And what will they be findin'?'

'Not a blessed thing.'

Paddy Gogarty removed his steel helmet and rubbed his carrot-red hair with his fingertips.

'Flower-baskets?' he asked.

'Flower-baskets, Paddy, If you can rig them.'

'The sand-mole routine?' said Paddy Gogarty.

'Snow-mole,' said Oram.

'In daylight?'

'The Germans aren't going to wait until dark.'

'You're thinkin' they'll be takin' Roshtan soon?'

'It's inevitable,' Oram answered. 'Roshtan is below the effective range of most of the partisans' weapons.'

'But,' said CSM Gogarty, 'if the krauts could be stopped, their formation broken, a half-mile further up, in open ground, sure they'd be sittin' ducks. An' if they was to be caught there come dark, no sayin' what those Russian cutthroats would get up to.'

'And we'd have gained a day.'

'How would we get the holes dug without bein' seen?'

'Camouflage capes.'

'A tunnel?'

'Why not?'

'It's a job for a brave man, sir.'

'Oh, we're all that, aren't we, Paddy?'

The Irishman hesitated. 'If a tank stopped with the flower-basket on her, stopped over the hole, like—'

'The odds against that happening are really awfully short.'

'How many flower-baskets?'

'Six at least, if you can rake up the necessary materials.'

'We'll need to cut out now, major, to get the work done in time.'

'Yes. I'll leave the Deke in charge here.'

'What'll you tell Captain Deacon, sir?'

'The truth, of course,' said Major Oram. 'Now, Paddy, what do you need?'

'My head examined,' said Paddy Gogarty.

*

By five minutes to noon the original parachute drop of fourteen SAS officers and men had been reduced to nine.

Corporal Wilkes had taken a bellyful of shrapnel from a rifle grenade while switching positions along the dyke. He had died, screaming, before the Russians could bring down a stretcher party to pull the young man out. With Major Oram and CSM Gogarty gone back up the hill to prepare a surprise package for the Germans and with Buz and the Red colonel not yet arrived, Deacon's unit now numbered five; four snipers and a very frustrated captain.

The only thing to be said for it was that chance had left the four best marksmen in the regiment alive and well and working the wall at Roshtan. P.B. had no patent on skill with a rifle. Each man was expert in outguessing the encroaching guns, ducking streams of vivid white tracers, scuttling to new emplacements and remaining there just long enough to pick off any krauts who showed themselves between the teeth of the Tigers.

Obviously the German commanders had decided not to risk a flanking manoeuvre with unprotected men. Cannon-fire from the tanks' 8.8 cm guns was sparse and not particularly accurate. The prong of the German advance was too close to the dyke to permit direct shelling from the artillery at Dzera and the field pieces were even now being manhandled into the town street to join the tail of the column that straggled up the highway.

Deacon had the distinct impression that, come what might, the Waffen-SS would not turn back but would grind their way inexorably to the summit of Baku-Ashran. But the terrain was tough for tanks which weighed upwards of fifty tons and the rate of advance was slow.

Digging crews, in white smocks and snowshoes, made excellent targets for Lee Enfields.

Though Roshtan might appear to have been obliterated by flames and high-explosive and, latterly, by the Tigers' MGs, Deacon's tiny unit, well strung out and acting independently, not only survived the last hour of the morning but appeared to have checked the advance.

Seven hundred yards downhill from the shattered dyke, the tanks heaved to a standstill.

Apparently a lead tank had suffered engine failure.

It took the panzer engineers forty minutes to coax the brute into motion once more, during which period the SAS snipers increased their 'bag' considerably, evening up the odds to approximately thirty to one. But the captain was mindful of the partisans crouched behind the bulwarks of the pass, of Safaryan's unexplained absence; he had a fishy feeling that the Red colonel was biding his time and would eventually appear with reinforcements. Whether any of the SAS men currently in Roshtan would be around to cheer was anybody's guess but, having seen Boris Safaryan in action, Deacon doubted it.

In due course, the disabled Tiger was backed off the line of advance and the leading pair rebalanced. The column shook itself and came grinding on.

At length Deacon was obliged to sound the whistle to summon the five to retire to the emplacement that he had selected for their final fling.

Deacon ran back from the dyke to a mound of rubble which protected a deep trough. To his right the village church had been reduced to a pyre of timber which smoked in the sunshine like a compost heap. Zigzagging like waterbeetles on a pond, Owens and McIndo crossed the flat from the ruins. Each man carried a Bren, a rifle and a sack of grenades. In the trough – a community sewer – snow had laid a thick white carpet, pocked by debris. The SAS men slithered into position and, in seconds, had the Brens on bipods, assembled and ready to fire.

One foot on the rubble, Deacon blew his whistle again. He fired a couple of rounds from his service revolver.

Peters was next in; a pea-headed comical-looking Lancastrian, tall and raw-boned, tough as steel. He had 'walked home' from desert raids on three separate occasions, a total distance of four hundred and seventy miles, across desert wastes that even Arab traders avoided.

'Eyyy, captain, what a reet crock o' shit we've landed in this time,' he declared.

102

'There, Peters, over there. When I give the word, you're first away. Keep on your right and the hill will protect you. Did you park your skis where I told you?'

'Over by that there rock, sir.'

'Good chap.'

Only two men defended the dyke now, Corporals Kemble and McNair. They blazed away with Brens, short bursts, hustling, weaving, shifting, firing again.

The big wind had ruined everything. With a full detachment and proper weapons, the SAS could have held this place for ever.

Nothing much came over the dyke now.

The blue sky was seamless, the sound of the tanks' advance continuous. Range to the enemy could be no more than three hundred yards. There would be no pause. Advance to Contact would be the order.

Deacon glanced back at the avenue of escape. His original notion that he would hold Roshtan to the last man had been abandoned. It had been nothing but a silly impulse to show the damned Russians that the British were courageous too. No more of that bloody nonsense. Five lives were valuable. He would not throw them needlessly away.

The runnel, in deep snow, went up for a thousand feet. The banks were packed hard where the wind had driven snow against solid rock. Ski-climbing would carry his men out of the Roshtan swiftly enough to give them a chance if P.B. and he made a nuisance of themselves for as long as possible.

Tanks first, of course; the first thing he would see would be the snouts of the Tigers. When they slammed down over the dyke, it would be time to cut out.

It did not unduly surprise Deacon when Kemble fell back from the dyke and, clutching his left shoulder, lurched towards the trough. Deacon went over the rubble and brought Kemble in.

The wound was a complication, though not as bad as it looked; a bullet had plucked through the crown of Kemble's shoulder. Deacon supported him over the mound.

Kemble shouted, 'Flankers. They got flankers on us, captain.'

'What do you mean?'

'About twenny-five or thirty of the buggers gone wide.'

'Didn't you fire at them?'

'Got some, but not all.'

'Oh, hell!'

Deacon hadn't counted on a flank attack.

The Jäger, of course! Bound to be Jäger troops doing the dirty work, tackling the snow-drowned gully that rose by the side of the plateau. Had he pulled back too early? Should he have held the dyke until the tanks were on top of him, until his men could spit through the visors? Surely the panzers had twigged that the defence was made of tissue paper and that Roshtan was theirs for the taking? Four Tigers would be enough. The danger was that the Jäger would find a fast route on to the mountainside, gain a high ground position which would make escape impossible.

'Owens, get Kemble out of here. Peters, McIndo, hold it here until I give you the signal, then go. Don't hang around. Go,' Deacon yelled.

'Right, skipper.'

'Kemble, can you ski?'

'On me 'ead, if I 'ave to.'

Deacon scrambled over the rubble once more and ran straight to the dyke.

Left of the village, the mountainside seemed smooth and impassive. He wondered how the Jäger would tackle it. Crampons and ice-steps? They didn't need to gain more than a couple of hundred feet over the plateau on which the village was perched. Two hundred feet would grant them command of the routes to the summit. Four gunners would be enough to seal Deacon's escape hatch.

Panting, Deacon flung himself down by the Scots corporal.

'What's happening?'

'Not bloody much.'

Six, not four, Tigers had been manoeuvred into rank across the width of the snow skirt. Fluffy snow glistened in the afternoon sun and already, away across the Dzera valley, there was that powdery blue smudge that said that dusk was not too far off. Four and a half hours until nightfall. By no stretch of the imagination could Roshtan be held until the stars came out. Fifteen minutes at most would see the Jäger in position.

'Where did the climbers go?' Deacon asked.

'Off left. In yon gully,' P.B. answered.

'The panzers are obviously waiting until their climbers reach an overlook position to chop down our retreat,' said Deacon.

'When the tanks come, we're fuckin' sunk,' P.B. remarked.

'Oh, damn it! Let's get out of here.'

'Haud on,' said P.B. 'Give the lads a chance.'

Deacon let his breath out and looked back at the rubble mound.

'But if I signal them to quit, P.B., we'll be left with no rear cover.'

'Well, you said it was t'be just you an' me.'

'I didn't expect—'

'Too bloody late,' said P.B.

Before Deacon could pick up the target, the Scot whirled and fired the Bren.

The Jäger trooper, dressed in white and hooded like a friar, had just attained a snow bluff to the left of their position. He died there, touching his forehead to the snow as if he had paused to pray.

'He's roped,' Deacon cried. 'So he's the leader.'

The captain fired his warning shot.

Peters and McIndo, crouched low as lizards, slithered back from the rubble wall into the trough and disappeared.

P.B. squeezed a burst from the Bren.

The Jäger trooper, who had scrambled over his dead comrade's back, raised himself to fire.

P.B.'s shots caught him in the chest. The soldier's body fell with a listing motion that carried it down the gully out of sight. There were cries, loud cries; then the body came into view once more, three hundred feet below, as it skated out of the gully mouth and came to rest close to the Tigers.

The tanks shuddered, growled, and started forward as if the arrival of a dead man had roused their anger. Six in line they advanced, tipping gradually into the slope. Blown snow furrowed back from the mantels. Trailing panzers clawed over it, like beached swimmers.

P.B. fired on them. This time he drew an immediate, ferocious response.

Bullets spat off rocks, *thocked* into snow cake.

Two more Jäger troopers nervously elbowed their way out of the gully. Bellies to the snow, they showed little except the black snouts of their MP 40s, abruptly budded with flame.

P.B. waited no longer. Instinct overrode courage. He rammed the barrel of the Bren into his left elbow, bracing the butt plate against his hip, and flayed the bole of snow above as he crabbed across open ground towards the protection of the trough.

Deacon ran too, firing his revolver in random fashion, head turtled between his shoulders.

Directly behind the SAS soldiers, half a dozen hand grenades sent up a curtain of dirty snow, blasting a hole in the crust of the dyke.

The noise of Bren and MP fire deafened Deacon. The untidy shock wave from the grenades hurled him, dazed, on to his knees.

'This way, for Chrissake,' P.B. yelled.

Corporal and Bren-gun seemed to be welded together.

No retaliatory fire came from the mountainside but, as he rose to run again, Deacon caught sight of a tiny jet-black dot, like a horsefly, high in the air.

The grenade fell short but the fountain of debris sprayed him, blinding him for an instant. Deacon staggered, yawed to his left and fell. Blearily he saw the mound. P.B. on his knees on it was struggling with a jammed Bren-gun.

Jäger troops wormed over the snow. Spread-eagled they raised their rifles and sub-machine-guns.

Deacon scrambled to his feet – an excellent target – dived forward and shoulder-rolled into the trough.

Owens and Kemble, on skis, were well up the runnel, going

106

strong by the look of it. Peters and McIndo were not far behind them. The Jäger troops hadn't spotted the escape route yet.

'Where's your fuckin' gun?' P.B. bawled at Deacon.

'I – I've – lost it.'

'Sweet Jesus!'

Rapping the catch with the heel of his hand, P.B. failed again to secure the jammed magazine. Tiny droplets of blood flew in all directions as, on his knees in the trough, the Scot applied the science of brute force to the Bren's recalcitrant mechanism.

Deacon crawled along the depression in search of a weapon – a Bren, a Tommy gun, a damned stone to throw, anything to buy them breathing space.

At any moment the Jäger troops would fan out across the mountainside, station eight or ten gunners in ideal positions to bring down Owens, Kemble, Peters and McIndo.

'Fuck it, fuck it, fuck the fuckin' thing,' P. B. McNair shrieked, hurled the useless Bren-gun away from him and swung the Lee Enfield from about his shoulder. *'Get out of here, Deke.'*

'Both of us.'

'Naw!'

'Yes!'

P.B. straightened and, balanced on his tail bone, supported the rifle in the vee of his knees. He fired three shots before the rifle, too, packed in.

'Now,' Deacon shouted. *'Now will you chuck it?'*

Together they rose and ran.

The first of the Tigers loomed over the dyke. Crushing stones beneath its massive tracks, it crashed on to the plateau. Five others swarmed up on its flanks. Foot soldiers, yelling like demons, flooded the avenues between the tanks.

On the mountainside above, only fifty yards away, Jäger marksmen, kneeling for best angle, took careful aim.

There was no cover, only snow.

Sweating, slithering on the slope, Deacon fixed his attention on the toes of his boots, driving them hard into the snow, waiting for pain to envelop him, and then darkness.

He never saw the bullets or, with fear drumming in his ears, heard the glassy echo of the rifle shot as it sang out across the mountainside.

Cold mountain air dried the sweat on Buz's upper lip and the saliva in his mouth. Tongue clamped between his teeth, hands balled into fists, he wanted to order the girls to squeeze the triggers. But he knew it would be fatal to intervene. For Deacon and P.B., this was the crunch. Their lives depended now upon the skill of a couple of Russian kids; and on Buz's ability to keep anxiety in check just a few moments longer.

A breeze ruffled the white canvas snow screens on their white-painted posts. Not much of a wind, maybe, but enough to drag the bullets an inch or two off line. There would be no second chances.

Jesus, how could Nina Safaryan remain so goddamned calm?

She was seated in the snow by Buz's side. In the kidskin ski-suit, she might have been resting on the terrace of a café in fashionable St Moritz instead of presiding over a fight to the death. She smoked a cigarette, a black Sobranie with a gold tip. She blew out a cloud of the fragrant smoke.

Directly below Buz and Nina, the girls were spread in a perfect firing position; slender legs, nice little fannies, an obscene daintiness about them, fists on the stocks of the Mannlicher 'scoped hunting rifles, slim fingers on the triggers; Natalya and Natasha hidden by the vents of the camouflage screen.

It didn't much matter if they were seen. The range was a thousand yards. None of the krauts would make that with accuracy, uphill.

In the deepest kink of the runnel, Owens and Kemble had reached safety. They could veer left now and wade up to the gate of the pass without danger from the Jäger guns. Peters and McIndo were struggling though. They looked, Buz thought, like manic ducks, the skis canted out, waddling as fast as they could.

It was Deacon and P.B. that Buz feared for. They were caught in the bowl below the buttress, beneath the German guns.

What the hell were the kids waiting for?

Tanks were lipping the ruins of the dyke, dumping into Rosh-tan. Buz watched panzer grenadiers pour out of the lanes between the tanks and dribble away into holes and pits. Still expecting resistance?

'Nina, for Chrissake?'

'Phissst!' The blonde hissed to silence protest.

It was like a nightmare, squatting there in bright sunshine on the slope of the mountain west of the pass, a grandstand seat from which to watch Jeff and P.B. scramble for dear life, watch helplessly while the Jäger troops found position and took aim.

Nina gave no order.

The crack of the Mannlichers sang out, a beautiful sound that bounced beautiful echoes across the head of the pass.

Twenty feet below him, Natalya and Natasha smiled.

Two Jäger were dead already.

Buz did not need binoculars to read the score. Again the Mannlichers boomed. Two more krauts slouched backwards into the gully. The rest, five in all, quit their cautious advance around the snow ledge and scrambled for cover.

Jeff and P.B. had hit the deck.

Buz gave a cheer and punched the sky in delight. 'Yeah-ha! Yeah-ha!'

With complete concentration and calculation, the two girls pumped bullets into the knot of retreating Germans on the snow ledge, killing three more.

'Yeah-HA! Yeah-HA! Yeah-HA!'

Jeff and P.B. were up and running; running like hell through the thickening drifts, wallowing on to harder ground where the stream that formed the runnel turned to pure ice. P.B. skidded on his ass, got up again, ran on. Deacon was right behind him, cutting out of the shadow of the mountain, east of the pass. Growing larger all the time, the pair forged across the snow skirt that would bring them safely to the highway's upper reaches.

The girls stopped firing. Cocking their heads, they chattered at each other, giggling happily. Nina offered them praise. They smiled over their shoulders at her and at Buz.

'Great shootin', kids.' Buz held up thumb and forefinger. 'Bull's-eye every time.'

A half-hour later, Buz greeted Deacon and P.B. by the side of the timber half-gate and shared with them the bottle of vodka and water that Nina had found to celebrate.

The party didn't last long for, wasting not one minute of the remaining hours of daylight, Waffen-SS panzers had filed the Tigers through Roshtan and the assault on Baku-Ashran had properly begun.

5 Baku-Ashran

Colonel Safaryan's peasant army assembled in the upper reaches of the valley of the Ganevis. Cooking fires pricked the wedges of purple shadow that sloped from the peaks and there was, in the camp, an air of excitement, almost of gaiety.

The SAS were surprised how few men there were among the partisans, until Nina explained that most able-bodied males had been conscripted into the Red Army. What was left was a motley collection of boys, girls, women and old men. Their weapons were primitive, mostly carbines and local Stings; Uncle Safaryan's acquisitions had been dispersed among the guardians of the pass, hard-core partisans. In all, there were no more than fifty men to stiffen the village army, plus Nina's Angels of Death.

Buz helped assemble the mortars that had been retrieved from the mountains further down the valley. Ammunition was woefully scarce and the defenders' first salvo was, of necessity, of short duration. The barrage, such as it was, gave the advancing Tigers no pause and, as shadows lengthened and the sun cooled, the tanks growled ponderously upwards, two abreast, inexorably devouring the highway beneath their steel tracks, dragging the long column of panzer grenadiers behind them.

Now that Colonel Safaryan had arrived on the scene, Vlad returned to the peasant camp. Communications were restricted to a couple of short-wave radios and an antiquated field telephone whose wire had been slung across the valley and zig-zagged down the deserted riverbed on three-foot stakes. Billeting was in long, low tents packed with mouldy straw which had been lugged up on horse-drawn sleds. The Safaryans' command HQ was set up in a square hut which stood, like a gypsy caravan, on an anchored sled in a bay of rock only fifty yards from the half-gate.

The movement of partisans and wheeled carts, in addition

to the sledges, churned the snow to brown slush which, with the onset of evening, froze rapidly and treacherously.

The SAS men who had fought in Roshtan and survived were resting in one of the long tents. Corporal Kemble had received medical attention and was being nursed, much to his disgust, not by one of Nina's girls but by a burly matron with a dark moustache, whose knowledge of English stretched only to three words – Eat, Drink, Sleep.

Snipers were worked into position on the snow ledges that overlooked the middle reaches of the pass, four of Nina's girls armed with the powerful 'scoped Mannlichers, among them.

The highway itself was deserted, a carpet of untrammelled snow which rolled upwards and wrinkled into the narrow summit. No gun emplacements, no ambuscades, no tank traps, no minefields, nothing appeared to impede the Germans' advance towards engagement at the half-gate.

Major Walter Oram and CSM Paddy Gogarty were invisible in their snow hole.

Colonel Safaryan had agreed at once to back the SAS major's scheme which, if successful, would surely prevent the panzers gaining ground suitable for a leaguer and halt them in an exposed position, vulnerable to guerrilla attack and within range of the mortars.

Safaryan quickly organized teams of raiders to inflict damage on the strung-out German column. Before that could be accomplished, of course, Oram and Gogarty must work their tricks with the flower-baskets.

The trouble with planting men in snow holes, as Walter Oram explained, was that they might freeze to death before the enemy reached them. The solution to that little problem, however, was simple – mole tunnels.

Snow, Oram declared, was a much nicer substance than sand and, if you knew what you were about, snow could provide a saboteur with an ideal medium for his work. Once, he said, he had spent five days in a snow hole in the mountains of Greenland and had not only survived but had actually rather enjoyed the experience. Paddy Gogarty remained sceptical.

Short shovels, shoring staves and containers of high-explosive – in this case, Russian mines – was all the equipment required, plus an expert knowledge of snow textures and drift patterns.

Fifty tons of Tiger rolling over a stretch of snow created impaction of considerable depth. In Oram's opinion, the Germans would probably utilize steel girders, brought up and placed by their engineers. The girders would be laid laterally across the highway in spots where the slope indicated that there might be soft drifts.

'So what do we scout for, Paddy?' Oram asked.

'A soft drift, sir,' Gogarty answered.

In camouflage suits, working behind snow screens, the pair soon found an ideal site for the tunnel. They dug inwards through the base of a drift from the shoulder of the highway. Even if their activity was noticed by the Germans, who were somewhat occupied in taking the Roshtan dyke, it was improbable that its purpose would be deduced. As Oram had predicted, the drift was composed of unlayered snow. Only along the lean of the rock step were the crystals large and icy. Ten yards in length, the mole tunnel was shored at intervals with planks braced between the ell of the rock step and the ground.

In due course, four of Nina's girls struggled downhill with the mines that Safaryan's officers had doctored to Gogarty's specifications. Simple fuses had been replaced by delayed action spring devices which could be set for short or long duration a moment before insertion and activation; twelve mines containing a total of one hundred and fifty pounds of TNT, fuse elements brought in a separate rucksack. Oram and Gogarty slid into the mouth of the tunnel. The girls covered over it with brushwood and caked snow. The snowscreens were furled and taken away.

Wrapped in blankets and wearing huge sheepskin gloves to keep their hands from becoming numb, the major and the CSM settled down for a long wait.

Mines and fuses had been pushed along the tunnel and placed below the two adjacent blow-holes that Oram had skilfully excavated, man-width bores that did not quite breach the surface of the drift in the dead centre of the track.

'What if the krauts don't get this far tonight, major?'

Oram blinked on his battery torch and consulted his wristwatch.

'If they aren't here in four hours, we'll pop out for a recce; it'll be dark by then, of course.'

'Mary and Joseph! I hope they come soon.' Gogarty clamped his teeth together to stop them chattering. 'I used to think sand was bad, but—'

'Oh, they'll come,' Oram muttered. 'They'll want to roll at least six of those brutes on to the upper highway to give long-gun cover to their foot soldiers. In fact, if the night stays clear, I wouldn't be surprised if they slot support trucks behind the first column of tanks. Heavily guarded against guerrilla attacks, of course. But they will be rather keen, I fancy, to lay up close to this little *mauvais pas* and have a strongish force on the broad part of the track above it.'

Paddy Gogarty trusted the major's judgement; the old man was seldom wrong.

'Yes, sir,' Gogarty said. 'Sure, and it's a grand night for a bit of fun, any roads.'

'Sure and it is, Paddy,' the major replied with a chuckle and, puffing his unlit pipe, fell silent, listening for the first telltale creak and rumble of the giant steel tracks on the snow.

Standing by the half-gate, Deacon and Buz Campbell watched the German advance. Neither the captain nor the sergeant knew precisely where Walter and Paddy were hidden. They were tense and strained with the effects of the events of the past couple of days and argued snappishly.

'Christ, how did I know the idiot colonel was gonna drag me round with him?' Buz demanded.

'You weren't manacled, were you?' said Deacon. 'You couldn't bring yourself to leave the ladies, I suppose?'

'It wasn't like that,' said Buz. 'Nina had nothing to do with it, for Chrissake! At least we found the weapons, some of them. Shit, we've done a fair job so far. What's your beef?'

114

'Given a modicum of proper support, we could have held the village until darkness fell,' Deacon said.

'Yeah? This ain't friggin' Salisbury Plain, Jeff. You can't whistle up tin soldiers just when you want them.'

'I could have used you down there.'

'Jesus! What good would I have done? One more gun.'

'Oh, you're probably right,' said Deacon, capitulating wearily. 'I'm feeling decidedly abandoned. The weather's perfect. Holms has had ample time to turn the crews around and despatch a rescue mission. I have the strong suspicion that we've been officially dropped in the manure.'

'Holms wouldn't do that, not without good reason.'

'I'm not at all sure we were needed in the first place. Safaryan seems to have it all pretty well organized. Girls, indeed! Olympic athletes. Cocktail cigarettes, American ground coffee and Mannlicher rifles. Blondes in ski-suits.'

'She's okay, Jeff.'

'Smitten?'

'Hell, no! But she's okay. It was her girl snipers got you out of Roshtan in one piece, remember.'

'I wonder why "her girls" didn't *hold* Roshtan.'

'You said yourself it wasn't possible without heavy artillery.'

'Safaryan has something up his voluminous sleeve,' said Deacon. 'There's more to our presence here than meets the eye.'

'Nope,' said Buz Campbell. 'I can't go with you on that one. You've seen the size of his so-called army. The dregs. Peasants, is all. The girls may be hot shit, Jeff, but the rest of the collection ain't no match for the Waffen-SS in full cry.'

'Yes, it's the tanks,' said Deacon. 'I admit I am very leery of the tanks.'

'Oram and Paddy'll settle their hash.'

'If such a scheme had been put forward by anyone other than Walter, I'd have tried to quash it.'

'It won't seem so crazy if it works,' said Buz.

'All right, we stop four or six tanks. We delay the advance for what – half a day. The Germans are quite strong enough to sustain thrust. They can't be *that* short of fuel and ammo, otherwise they wouldn't have begun the advance at all, even

115

with a Red Army division behind them, cutting off their retreat.'

'Yeah.' Buz folded his arms and surveyed the column as it emerged on to the apron at the back of the ruined village. 'They know they can make it – if they just keep coming.'

'And if they do breach the pass – tomorrow or Sunday – Hitler will pull two or three divisions from the front elsewhere and paradrop them in here.'

'But no tanks.'

'Don't be an idiot, Buz. You've seen the Ganevis valley. It's a perfect assault base.'

'Except when the wind blows.'

'He's no fool, Adolf. Once the panzers are on the road to the Caspian, with the last real resistance behind them, he'll throw everything he can into an attack on the oilfields.'

'He might be too late.'

'It will become a race, one which the Germans stand a good chance of winning.'

Buz Campbell said, 'Not while Boris has his health and strength.'

'Changed your tune, haven't you?'

'Maybe.'

Gloomily, Deacon studied the highway below. 'We can pick off only so many of them, Buz. After that—'

'Hey, Jeff, are your scared?'

'Of course not. I'm cold and fed up, that's all. Very, very cold and very, very fed up.'

'Go back to Boris's wagon,' said Buz. 'I'll let you know when anything happens.'

'No.'

'It's Walter, ain't it? Walter and Paddy?' said Buz, quietly. 'It's got fuck-all to do with Boris. You're worried about our guys down there.'

'Aren't you? Worried?'

'Stiff,' Buz Campbell admitted.

The 'flower-basket' had been invented by the late Lieutenant Powys-Prescott of SAS 'B' Group Desert Raiders, a forward-

116

front outfit of some thirty officers and men whose exploits remained a mystery even to Colonel Holms. The flower-basket was a simple device, the result of necessary improvisation, infinitely variable according to what sort of explosives were available. Basically the flower-basket was a cradle of stout wire with four hooks attached to its circular framework. Into the basket went slow-fuse mines, incendiaries, plastics, stick dynamite, or even, more than once, merely a handful of grenades wrapped to a timer and coil.

Flower-baskets had first been used on the road between Gehares and El Hadabah near the 'crossing line' on the edge of the Qattara Depression. Powys-Prescott and Walter Oram had been returning from a reconnaissance and had run into a German convoy, eight of Rommel's light tanks, protecting a score of soft-skinned supply trucks. All that Powys-Prescott and Oram had on hand were anti-personnel mines; even two SAS officers who had been in the desert for six weeks, one way and another, had not taken quite enough sun to tackle the Afrika Korps single-handed. But the prize had been just too meaty to pass up. Powys-Prescott had come up with the brilliant suggestion that they drive on ahead and set up a little bit of bother for the enemy which was, after all, what they were paid to do.

The first sand mole tunnel was hardly more than a shallow scoop in the centre of the road. In it the intrepid, not to say foolhardy, officer lay at full length, protected by a panel unbolted from the jeep, and a couple of feet of sand. Four flower-baskets on slow fuses were in the scoop with him and as the tanks rolled overhead, the lieutenant hooked a basket on to whatever protrusion he could reach, usually the front drive sprocket or leaf springs. The tanks had rumbled on along the track into the darkness, followed by the trucks. The last half-dozen trucks hadn't passed over the horizontal lieutenant when the tanks blew up; four decent little explosions which actually blew the decks and caused so much damage that the tanks had to be abandoned. Not content with his bag of four PzKpfw IIs, Powys-Prescott had wriggled from his coffin in the middle

117

of the track, crept back down the line beneath the halted trucks, ramming a steel spike through the exposed tops of the plated petrol tanks. Finally, he bobbed a grenade along the grit, rolled out from under the last truck and ran like hell for the spot of darkness where he hoped Oram would be waiting with the jeep's engine ticking over and the bonnet pointed towards safety.

On that occasion, Walter Oram had been waiting and the pair had got away unscathed. Next afternoon they had sneaked back to gloat over the carcasses and officially record the degree of damage caused by the newly devised weapon.

During the following three or four months, Oram had lain in sand holes a dozen times. He professed to enjoy it as much as Powys-Prescott evidently did, but, in fact, regarded the technique as roughly akin to playing Russian roulette with a half-loaded revolver.

In the end, Powys-Prescott had become a little too daring. He had died – horribly – when an armoured personnel carrier to which he had just attached a basket loaded with 20 lb of HE on short fuse backed over his trench and, before he could wriggle away, exploded, blowing the lieutenant's head, literally, to pulp.

After that, use of Powys-Prescott's infamous flower-baskets was outlawed by Holms and other SAS commanders and the technique fell into abeyance – until, that is, Major Walter Oram revived it far from the eyes of the high brass, in the heights of the Caucasus.

'Here they come, Paddy. Do you hear them?'

'Sure an' I do, sir.'

'Please sit absolutely still.'

'I will, major, I will.'

With his fingertips, Oram brushed away a flake or two from the snow that had been plastered over the side exit. It was still, visibly, daylight. He consulted his watch: a few minutes to four o'clock.

The din of the Tigers' approach was suddenly loud, like prolonged thunder. The panzers, pushing on fast, were not checking the track for mines. The Tigers would be almost

118

impervious to standard anti-tank mines buried in snow. The weight of their tracks and thick armour gave them abnormal protection. He cocked his head, heard the guttural conversation of foot soldiers only fifty or sixty yards from the rock step. Engineers running out with support beams? He couldn't see them, of course. The grenadiers were apprehensive, afraid of snipers. An NCO gave them a tongue-lashing, urging them to get on with the job. There was a sudden volley of covering fire, so close that the rifles might have been fired in the tunnel itself.

Oram tapped Paddy on the shoulder. The CSM dropped to his belly and slithered along the tunnel into darkness, left hand extended to feel for the mines.

Oram followed.

Crumbs of snow plopped from the tunnel roof. But there was no strain at all on the planks yet. Oram hoped that his calculations were correct, that the steel beams would take enough weight to leave the tunnel open. If the planks snapped and the tunnel collapsed, he and Paddy would be trapped; smothered or shot, depending on how close to the surface they were.

The major flicked on his pocket torch.

Paddy had gone on, pushing six mines ahead of him into the opening of the second bore shaft. Snow was coming down in lumps but there was no real impaction as yet. Oram could hear little now; no voices. He judged that it would take the sappers three or four minutes to bed the tank-width girders and make them secure. The purpose of the girders was not, after all, to provide a climbing bridge but only to distribute the weight of the tanks across a larger area of snow.

Reaching out, Oram shook Paddy by the boot, a signal for the Irishman to enter the second shaft and chimney his way up it. Oram picked up a mine and stuffed it into the pouch-like breast of his snow jacket. Very heavy; twenty pounds or more. He grunted, stifled the sound and stuck his knees into the yielding walls of the shaft. He hoisted himself up it in three strong movements, up to the little steeple where a mere six inches of snow capped the bore.

Strained by the awkward manoeuvres, his old bones cracked

as he worked off his gloves with his teeth and let them fall between his knees to the bottom of the shaft. Of necessity, the shafts were very tight. Once the girders were in place, however, and the first tank bedded them down, the bore shafts would be safe enough. With great care the major extracted the mine and pushed it into the snow on a level with his chest. He climbed down the shaft again and brought up another Russian pie-dish. He placed four in this way, two at chest level, two half-way up, where he could reach them by doubling between his knees. Last of all, he brought up the fuses.

Strange waxy light filtered through snow, enough for him to read the coding stamped on the metal cases. He groped in the tunnel wall and found the heavy wire baskets that he had planted earlier in the afternoon. They looked, he thought, like chip fryers. It was all very easy, even in poor light and confinement, to slip one of the pie-dishes into a wire basket. Supporting the basket between his chest and the shaft wall, Oram fished out a slow fuse device and fitted it neatly into the well at the heart of the mine. With great care he attached a ring to the arming plug and, with his pinkie, cocked it up through the aperture where the pressure plate would normally have been.

Oram held the mine flat on his left hand and waited.

Seconds later the first of the Tigers crossed the snow step.

Oram felt as if the sound alone would crush him, though the pressure was really surprisingly light. The steel beams did, in effect, spread the enormous tonnage of the beast. Even so, the major cowered involuntarily, drawing down his head and hunching his shoulders as the tracks rattled and gabbled over him and the beams slapped into the breast of the drift.

Blinded by loose snow, Oram shook his head and scooped at the snow plug. He punched his fist up through the snow and, groping round the angle of the girder, scraped away a hole large enough to take his shoulders and head and, of course, the mine.

The second Tiger was on him almost at once, the track only inches from his head. The depression of the girder was tremendous. Obliged to hurry, he tugged out the arming pin with his teeth and thrust the live mine upwards. The wire hooks

120

jutted towards the Tiger's torsion bars only inches above his face, like a huge, ornate ceiling. The underside of the tank was spotlessly clean, as if polished up by zealous mechanics. The gear box, however, was slick with diesel oil. He stabbed the basket upwards, felt it hook, catch and swing away from him as the tank tracks bit on the girders and chewed into the rock step. For an instant the major was staring up at an empty sky. He swivelled, looked back, saw a third tank closing but – happily – no accompanying soldiers; also a glimpse of Paddy's head protruding from the second shaft an arm's length away. The major dipped, unshelved his second mine, put it in its cradle, armed it and returned to the surface.

Even numbers – two, four, six and eight – Paddy had three, five, seven, nine. If, for any reason, the column checked its run on the rock step, Paddy and he would drop to the bottom of the tunnel and shoot out of the side exit, arming any mines they could reach without delay. The fuses were set for six-minute intervals. The baskets should hug close enough to the tank bodies not to be dislodged by the jump over the step; in theory, at least.

Oram worked fast now, his fingers extraordinarily nimble. He planted a mine on the fourth tank and on the sixth. He was beginning to imagine that he and Paddy might even get away with it. By God, if they did, he would buy the CSM a crate of champers back in Cairo and they would toast the memory of Powys-Prescott until neither of them could stand up.

He went up with the last mine on his hand like a silver tray, a hot little smile of satisfaction creasing his mouth.

He lifted his head through the hole.

An SS panzer grenadier shot him through the side of the neck.

Oram felt blood spurt out. He jerked the mine's arming ring, thrust the basket away, knocked his knees together and slid downwards just as the grenadier fired again.

Oram hit the bottom of the shaft twelve feet below. He was already beginning to black out through shock and loss of blood from the blast wound. Only the narrow, upright shaft kept him from pitching insensible to the ground. His knees sagged. He felt some great creature claw and maul at his feet. Was he being eaten alive by a snow mole, chewed into its bone-white mouth? He began to shout, to flap his arms. Could snow moles be scared away like sharks?

'Major! Mary 'n' Joseph, let go, sir.'

Paddy! Good old Paddy Gogarty! Best CSM in the British Army, any army, the world, the whole blasted universe.

Oram hung from the shaft, buckled legs blocking the horizontal tunnel and the CSM's escape.

'Paddy, old chap?'

The CSM was hauling at him. The major let himself yield, slip down the shaft to the tunnel. Flopping out flat, flat enough for Paddy to crawl over him, he closed his eyes.

'Oh, Jasus, Jasus!' Paddy moaned.

Breath in the major's lungs was as thick as custard. He expelled it, vomiting a splash of blood, sucking it in again when he inhaled. He could feel the damned, sticky stuff plastered over his moustache. Weakly he raised his arm to wipe it away.

Paddy had him by the webbing belt and was dragging him along the tunnel under the planks.

All hell back there; a solid rain of lead.

A grenade'll do the trick, boys, one tiny, jerry hand-grenade.

Blood accumulated in Oram's throat. He retched, jerking, thumping his brow against the last plank. CSM Gogarty was climbing all over him, push-pulling him. He felt the sweet, clean, snow-scented air of the high mountains on his face, glimpsed a sky of lapis lazuli, felt the rip of the brushwood screen as Paddy pull-pushed him clear of the tunnel.

And then, chaps, there was a big bang. What a bang, I tell you. Best and biggest bang I ever did see. Knew what they were doing with slow fuses, those stolid Russians. Bang to the second. *Bang. Bang. Bang.* Limp as kelp, the major sprawled on his belly, head down, suffocating on his own blood, while the German Tigers were disembowelled and the poor grenadier who had accidentally stumbled on the moles screamed and fell, left foot blown off just below the knee.

'Paddy,' said Oram, quite lucidly, 'I'm a gonner. Take off.'

A spray of fire from MP 28s, however, had finished Paddy Gogarty seconds before. He lay motionless five yards downhill.

So Major Walter Oram, the British Army's first and last snow mole, died alone, with the soft roar of a fourth Powys-Prescott special dinning in his ears and twenty-three German bullets buried in his head and chest.

Extract from the War Diary of Generalmajor Erich Münke

I had waited behind, when the column crept out of Roshtan, to see my boys safely off the mountain. We had five wounded, in addition to those killed by the snipers. I wanted to offer them a word of cheer and the assurance that they would not be left to fall into the hands of the Russians. Two were in a bad way, one of them calling for a priest. We did not have a priest. Instead, I found a Lutheran preacher who had somehow convinced himself that this was a Holy War and had taken a commission in the Waffen-SS. Captain Vogler was his name. He had enough humanity left in him to stay by the boy's side until he passed away. The other wounded men I left to the care of the medical corps with the assurance that they would be found places in one of the trucks and brought up with the column when the pass was breached.

When the pass was breached? Would the pass ever be breached? After all, had not a mere handful of Britishers kept us out of Roshtan and extracted a heavy toll in German lives for final entry?

By now I had lost one third of my strength. I did not share Gord's fanatical faith in the triumph of armour, however weak the Russian defences appeared to be in numbers and fire power. But Gord was determined. He had his Tigers crash on, refusing to listen to my suggestion that we leaguer for the night in Roshtan and allow the men to rest.

After argument, however, Gord permitted me to hold back the remains of my Gebirgstruppen, to bring them forward as a unit only when ten of the Tigers had passed through at Roshtan and struck up the winding highway.

To me it was folly to string out the column in such a manner, so close to nightfall. But Oberführer Gord was, by now, a man possessed. It was certainly true that Roshtan had been held only by a handful, that the SS Intelligence gatherers' belief that the Russians were without artillery gained credit from our examination of the village: six corpses in the uniform of British Special Air Service, and not a single Russian. Not a mortar, an anti-tank gun or field piece was to be found.

If it had been left to me, I would have sent my boys ahead, stealthily moving in units of four or six to keep them out of that lethal crossfire. I would have tried to slip them over the pass without direct confrontation. It may not have worked but it would have been, I believe, less wasteful than charging straight up the highway.

So it proved.

The 'indestructible' Tigers, which Gord claimed were immune to ground mines, were crippled by a handful of primitive bombs.

I was moving up the outside of the column on skis when the leading tanks blew up. Whoever laid the groundwork of the plan had chosen exactly the right place, on the crest of a rock step where the highway was flanked by a sheer wall of rock, some fifty feet in height and, on the right, by a deep bowl. There was no hope of by-passing the blockage which, with five Tigers already helplessly immobilized, would obviously cost us dear in time and lives.

It was not, however, the five crippled Tigers that worried the Oberführer so much as the unscathed tank at the head of the column. It had surmounted the rock step and gone on some two hundred yards across a flat, broad corner of the track. Now it was trapped and faced with the prospect of charging on alone or of making a fight of it where it stood; a devil's choice, really, for the Russians had planned it all down to the last detail.

It was at this juncture that they gambled their meagre resources and threw their men face-to-face into the fight. What they wanted was to possess that Tiger's long gun which, reversed into the summit of the pass by the timber gate, would be a fiercesome threat to our progress.

Five hundred yards from the head of the column, I got my boys down into the snow behind the tanks. Scrambling on to the bank, I trained my field-glasses on the fighting. If Gord was killed, I would be in sole command of the assault forces, a fact that was much in my mind.

The air was torn by the barking of the partisans' guns, by the snarl of MGs and the high-pitched whine of snipers' bullets, sounds that made the hair rise on the nape of my neck.

The Russians swarmed out of nowhere. Leaping across the ridges, they plunged down the snowfields left of the highway.

Some wore skis and shot off the ugly Stings as they flew, firing from the hip, braced against the fall line, squatting for balance then, without poles, jumping back into the descent. They were well spread out, like flies scattered by a wind, and they skimmed under their own shells towards our dithering Tiger without, apparently, a thought for survival. Peasants, women, young boys and old men, the people of the Caucasus went for the tank as if it was a carcass of meat and they were starving. When they fell – and many fell to Gord's panzer grenadiers – they did not lie still but dragged themselves upright and came on, limping forward; even when their injuries were mortal, they did not seem content to die peacefully but. writhed and yelled like demons frying in flames as they clawed through churned and bloody snow.

Our tank, the Tiger's long gun, that was their one objective.

The crippled tanks could not do much damage for, without power, the crews were obliged to crank the turrets by hand. What it was like within the steel coffins was hard to imagine. Two of the Tigers were on fire, roasting on under-flames, with mortar shells crumping all around.

I signalled to my boys and moved them up a hundred

yards or so and, bawling at them to keep down, I split
them into two crescents and ordered them to provide
covering fire to the panzer grenadiers who, spurred on by
the Oberführer, were endeavouring to check the landslide
of partisans.

I could make out Gord, even in diminishing light.
The Oberführer had every justification for getting himself
out of there and back down the column. What did I
know about tank warfare? He was ensnared by the action
for, like me, he had received his training on the battlefields
of Europe and not in the salons of Munich and Berlin.
But even to this day I cannot decide whether he
acted rightly or wrongly. Russians were almost there,
swooping from the pass itself, so spread out that there
seemed to be thousands of them.

The first wave reached the live Tiger and clambered
up on her, swarming over the sloped superstructure. Within
the vehicle, our Scharführer was still doing his job.

Engine roaring, he spun the tank round and round, the
turret rotating in full traverse, MGs blazing. The Russians
who were swept off the deck rose and flung themselves
once more upon the plating, those who weren't crushed
beneath the spinning tracks.

They could have crippled her with ease. But they
wanted her whole, particularly as they had no spare parts
and, presumably, no mechanics capable of repairing her.
Smoke bombs and bullets would overwhelm the crew
eventually. We had no hope of flinging a large force of
men over that rock step; Russian snipers saw to that,
snipers and mortars and the savage, suicidal partisans.

What did Waffen-SS Oberführer Gord do? He blasted
our trapped Tiger out of existence.

Five Tiger long guns slewed on to target in dreadful
unison; maximum range, a hundred and fifty yards.
Five Tiger long guns boomed and recoiled, boomed and
recoiled, boomed once more. Our tank, victim of equal
armament, burst into flames and, driven by another

calculated salvo, plunged over the track edge and performed
a ponderous somersault into the snow basin, flinging
streamers of flame and mangled corpses everywhere.

Astonished, my boys stopped firing. I bawled at them
and they stifled their horror and fell once more to
shooting while Oberführer Gord pulled back, pounding
many rounds into the crippled Tigers on the step ahead
of him. Ammo loads exploded. Tanks toppled over. One,
near the brink, followed its leader into the basin in spirals
of black smoke and petrol flames.

The Russians were caught now. They had lost their
focal objective and were naked in front of our grenadiers'
guns. A few came on, jabbering wildly, firing at random
until they were cut down. But the others, the sensible
ones, turned and set off up the slope again, up the
pallid ribbon of highway, while mortar and anti-tank
barrages intensified, doing damage to our soldiers but leaving
our precious armour unharmed.

Fearing that Gord would still press on, push through
the wreckage and risk bogging down, I waited for
his order. We were so strung out now that any sort
of night raid would have weakened us beyond measure.
Much to my relief, I received a verbal message from
Hauptsturmführer Schenken. The Oberführer's instructions
were plain – pull the column back to Roshtan for
regrouping.

With darkness crowding upon us, what else was there
to do? In Roshtan we could protect ourselves against
snipers and guerrillas and have hope of surviving the
night. Tomorrow, come what may, we must be fresh enough
to storm the pass again and this time to succeed in
taking it.

Naturally, I had no means of knowing that our task would
be made easy by an outside force, that the Führer himself
had finally taken a hand in the game.

*

Nina spent the night snuggled against Buz Campbell under a pile of blankets on the straw floor of the long tent. Whatever desire Buz felt for the woman, and it was at first considerable, waned at the sound of her weeping. Holding her head against his chest, he consoled her and encouraged her to talk.

It was the girls that Nina mourned, the little dead athletes. She had lost girls before, she said. Four had been taken prisoner near Kharsova on a raid against a troop train. Raped and tortured, their bodies had been tossed aside by the tracks when the Germans moved on.

Six other girls had died in a blizzard the previous March when returning from a patrol on the rim of the Mostuk Valley in Ossetia. And there had been more, dead and maimed, for her Angels had been active for many, many months, she said.

Nina could not, as Buz tried to do, make an equation out of it – ten dead Germans for every Georgian girl – nor could she bring herself to sustain hatred for the enemy. Recompense to the blonde woman took the form of denying the German will; that was her revenge. Unlike Boris, she had no 'official' existence and there were times, during the cold winter nights, when she felt as if she had become a phantom unconnected with reality. They were still down there, down in the bowl of the mountains, on the sad track, the cadavers of the dead and the bodies of the wounded; the Germans would allow no parties to retrieve them. It didn't matter, did it? They would all be dead before morning, all those who were left would be dead soon, for the war would last for ever.

Buz held her gently, stroking her hair, listening to her murmurous voice, so sad that it made him want to weep too.

Then, in due course, the woman and the man fell asleep.

When Buz wakened, it was still dark.

The iron stove had been lighted and gave a glimmering glow to the canvas. Nina seemed to be herself again, energetic and determined. She gave him coffee and bread and sat against his knees while he breakfasted, enjoying the silence that reigned over the mountains.

The girls were stirring, and SAS men, all bunked together in

128

the straw of the long tent. However willing Nina's girls may have been, Buz questioned if there had been much love-making under the blankets during the night. Exhaustion had chastened everyone.

After breakfast, Buz got up, splashed his face in the bucket of icy water by the tent door, dressed in his battle kit and took out the Vaughan shotgun.

Somehow he had the feeling that by the end of the day he would need it and all the shells he could stuff into the pockets of his combat suit.

At ten minutes after seven, he followed Nina outside. He found the peasant army moving up from its camp to the pass, taking positions for defence against an inevitable dawn assault.

Leaving Nina to muster her unit and position them at favourable sites on the mountainside, Buz found Deacon and P.B. at the forward gate. Crouched by the massive timber structure, they were smoking cigarettes and scanning the highway anxiously as it began to emerge from the darkness.

'What do we do now, Jeff?' Buz Campbell asked.

'Wait.'

'How long will it take them to get here?'

'Given a free run to the obstacles, a couple of hours at most.'

'What obstacles?'

'Safaryan's sappers bolstered the rock step with logs. Crude and probably not too effective. But it'll hold the Germans for a little while within mortar range. Apparently this new model tank can climb three feet of vertical obstruction without ramps.'

'And the krauts still have a couple of dozen in service?'

'Assuming no breakdowns or freeze-ups, yes.'

'What's the order for the lads?' asked P.B.

Since Major Oram's death, Deacon was in charge of the remnants of the SAS detachment. Deacon had discussed the situation with Safaryan. The Red colonel still believed that the pass could be held, even against an onslaught of tanks.

'We keep the gate,' said Deacon.

'Great!' said P.B. 'What about the lassies?'

'They will join us as soon as the tanks pass the corner. The villagers will be behind us, those that aren't in emplacements on the flanks.'

'What're the chances?'

'Actually, not too bad,' said Deacon. 'If we knock out three or four tanks, we might check the whole column again. Our defensive positions are reasonably well protected against the long guns, particularly as they don't have the best of elevations. Above all, we're sure that the Germans don't have a sufficient number of men to make a rush. If they elect to do that, we'll slaughter them.'

'Great!' said P.B.

'Wonder what the weather'll do?' Buz glanced at the sky. 'Cloud about. By the smell of it, it could snow.'

'It's clear enough to the north-west,' said Deacon. 'I doubt if we'll have snow before the first engagement.'

'What about thunder?' asked P.B. McNair.

'Thunder?'

'Aye. Listen.'

Hands on hips and ski-hood flung back, Deacon cocked his head and listened intently.

From Roshtan he could make out the whining of engines and other sounds of German preparation, more muted this morning, less sharp. But he heard nothing that P.B. might confuse with thunder.

'Yeah!' said Buz, quizzically. 'Yeah! Listen, Jeff, listen.'

Instinct told Buz what it was. Far from German-held air-strips, no one had given much thought to the possibility that the Luftwaffe would waste fuel on providing long-range air support. Somebody in German HQ had wakened up to the fact that the Caucasus might at last be breached.

The planes flew low along the Dzera, wing-tips seeming to brush the hillsides. There were a dozen in all, droning fiercely like angry hornets.

Behind the three SAS men, rose cries of confusion.

Safaryan's partisan officers, Vlad and Victor among them, tried to disperse the villagers, scatter them to shelter out of the funnel of the pass. Horse-sleds laden with ammo boxes were overturned. The orderly military-style organization of a minute ago dissolved in chaos.

Glancing back, Buz saw Nina lead her skiers away, sailing out of sight in the half-light, down the steep inner slope of the gorge. Nina's was the only group to get out before six Heinkel He 118s and six Stuka dive-bombers zoomed over Roshtan and, banking, dumped their bomb loads down the throats of the Allies trapped and helpless in the narrow pass.

The raid consisted of a combined formation run by Heinkels and Stukas, followed by an immediate return from the east, up the valley of the Ganevis, by the Stukas alone.

Crouched more or less where he had been standing when the planes hurtled out of the west, Deacon observed the fall of the bombs, black darts nodding and skimming from the wings, and saw spitting red machine-guns. But, deafened and shaken by the detonations, he did nothing to retaliate. A handful of partisans swung their guns towards the heavens and blasted away, but only until the first bombs fell, after which those who could still run exchanged valour for discretion and hid themselves as best they could among fallen rocks and flattened tents.

In all, the raid lasted six minutes.

In that period over fifty thousand pounds of explosive rained down on Baku-Ashran.

And then the planes were gone. Swinging north-west across the peaks towards the veil of cloud, they quickly vanished from sight of the survivors.

Tossing his singing head from side to side like a wounded bull, Deacon got to his feet and looked around for Buz and P.B. He found them pressed against the roots of the timber gate.

The gate had taken several direct hits. Jagged splinters had cartwheeled in all directions, bowling wickedly into clusters of villagers who had been caught on the summit of the pass, struggling with sleds and fear-crazed horses. One of the horses, a strong, young animal, had been impaled by flying timber. It was still bizarrely upright, propped like a lead model, the post protruding through its body, its hoofs in a lake of steaming

131

blood. The other horse had been punctured by a chain of metal shrapnel. It lay on its side, still roped into the shafts, snickering and pawing the air until, mercifully, it died.

Eight of the ten gun emplacements had been wiped out, mortars destroyed. Ammo dumps had gone up, adding to the damage. All the way back over the summit, the bodies of partisans and villagers were strewn, a grisly, groaning harvest of women and boys, young peasant girls and bemused old men who had been promised the thrill of killing a few German soldiers in exchange for their lives.

Deacon could hear their cries only faintly. He was deaf. He tapped his fingers briskly against his ears, as he had been taught to do, and was rewarded by a hollow drumming echo in the inner canals. In due course, minutes or hours, his hearing would return. He peeled off a mitten and explored his face with his fingertips. There was no wetness of blood. Even so, he felt as if his skin had been flayed from the bones by a scalding wind. Hordes of tiny, tinsel-like dots hovered before his eyes.

Buz was shouting at him.

Deacon pointed at his ears and shook his head.

'Can't hear a word,' he mouthed.

Buz gestured.

Wheeling, Deacon was confronted by the pathetic remains of the SAS paradrop detachment. Three soldiers, his comrades, were dragging themselves towards him, one upright, though bleeding, and two on all fours.

Deacon hurried to them, knelt.

'Kemble's dead,' said McIndo. He made a dumb show.

'And you? How bad is it?' Deacon shouted.

'Shot in the leg. Need a twister, sir. Splint too, maybe.'

McIndo's ski-suit was soaked with blood below the thigh of his left leg.

'Buz,' Deacon shouted. *'Buz, find medical help.'*

P.B. was by his side now, kneeling to support Owens who was clearly seriously wounded. The little corporal laid his comrade gently into the snow. There was blood all over Owens' groin and belly, and his combat jacket had been all but ripped off by blast.

'*Medics, medics, medics,*' Deacon screamed, ignoring stabs of pain in his ear-drums and behind his eyes. '*Where the devil are the medics?*'

He saw P.B. speaking, but could make out not a word.

He saw Owens speak too, cracked and blackened lips moving. He pressed his ear down but there was nothing, nothing audible, only tiny bubbles on the lips, perfect little domes, as if Owens was burping up port wine.

P.B. drew Deacon back.

'Peters ain't so good either, Jeff.'

'*What? I can't—*'

Peters had struggled into a sitting position, knees extended. He had both hands, bare, pressed against the flesh of his inner thighs, thumbs digging into the muscles. Across the material of the trousers, an inch or so above the tops of his boots, were two thick, tarry welts.

'Knobbled,' Peters said, and giggled. 'Knobbled like a bleedin' nag.' He giggled again. 'Can't feel a bleedin' thing down there. Not a bleedin' dicky-bird. Still got somethin' there, though, or me boots'ud fall off. Ain't that reet P.B.?'

'Aye, right,' P.B. answered.

Peters had been struck across the shins by a length of timber, unbarked, raw-edged and heavy. Within his trouser legs there was only a jelly of crushed bone and tissue, too contused to leak blood. The best surgeons in the world would not be able to save Peters' legs. If he did, somehow, survive the day, it was sure that he would never walk upright on his own pins again.

The young soldier giggled, closed his eyes, and sat patiently in the snow with his thumbs pressed into arteries, waiting to be told the worst.

Daylight had crept up the Ganevis.

The light was pearly, not brilliant as it had been yesterday and the day before.

'I'll stay with them, Jeff,' said P.B. 'You'd better find Safaryan. See what's happenin'.'

'*What?*'

P.B. made signs. Deacon nodded. He drummed on his ears again with his knuckles while Peters, eyes open, watched in amusement. There was a sudden sifting hiss inside Deacon's skull and he was beset by the hideous noises of suffering, by the crackle of burning wood and straw. In his nostrils was the reek of bombs, smoke and snow.

He got up.

McIndo said, 'If you can find me a twister, sir, I'd be much obliged.'

'I'll do what I can,' Deacon promised and, still dazed, walked woodenly away.

He felt very badly about the men, as guilty as if he had led them into this trap. It was just as bad for the villagers, of course. He noted, rather absently, the Russian wounded. He had no idea where he was going, what he was looking for. He walked towards the wreckage of the timber gate, stepping over debris, over the rag-doll corpses of Safaryan's warriors, through the dispersing wisps of smoke.

Visibility wasn't so hot this morining. Could barely make out the mountains behind Dzera now, though Roshtan was clear enough, even to the naked eye.

As he had expected, the damned Germans hadn't wasted a moment. They were roaring out of Roshtan now, thrusting up towards the pass, taking full advantage of the Luftwaffe air strike; a sprinkle of moderately small bombs; nothing gigantic which would leave insurmountable craters in the surface of the highway. Carcasses of tanks remained from last night's fracas. Bodies. Walter and Paddy would be among them. Somewhere. God, but the krauts were getting a shift on this morning. Vaguely Deacon wondered how they had kept the tanks from freezing, a perennial problem for panzers, how much fuel they had left and if they had succeeded in bringing a convoy of petrol trucks down the line. What would it be like to be a prisoner of the Waffen-SS? Would he be better off dead?

Boris Safaryan put a hand on his shoulder.

Deacon jumped and almost felled the Russian colonel with his fist.

'Medical help for my men,' Deacon shouted. 'Where is it? You're supposed to be in charge of this operation, aren't you?'

134

'Campbell found a doctor. One chap dies already. You give them chance?'

'How do I know what chance they have? What chance any of us have now? God, Safaryan, this whole operation is a bloody shambles.'

'We get to help, to Vasheli. Sledges out, wounded on them.'

'Wonderful!' said Deacon. 'How long will that take?'

'Some horse. One hundred, eighty miles.' Safaryan shrugged. 'Five days.'

'And how many will make it alive, do you suppose?'

'Stop, Deacon. That is chance. Only chance for them, your soldiers.'

'Safaryan, don't you realize that we're sunk? Don't you realize that the speed of a German tank is in the region of fifteen miles an hour? Once they roll through the pass, the Germans will head straight for this safe town of yours, this Vasheli, and that they will receive all sorts of support? In case it hadn't occurred to you, those planes were *ordered* here by somebody in the German GHQ, by bloody Adolf himself, for all I know. And there will be *more*, you can bet your boots, old man. *More* planes, *more* troops, *more* supplies.'

'But no petrol oil.'

Safaryan's rubicund cheeks were streaked with a sooty substance. Over his Red Army battledress he wore a bulky sheepskin coat, buttoned only at the collar. With a sweeping gesture of his arms he flung it back. He shot out one hand and gripped Deacon's chin. There was no friendliness in the touch. The fingers closed tightly, holding Deacon still.

'You, three soldiers. Me, two hundred to save.'

The colonel's eyes were fierce.

'Yes, all right. I accept that,' said Deacon, abashed. 'How many men do you have fit and willing to fight?'

'I not know.'

'My guess is fifty. And how much armament?'

'Stop. We save. You, me, Deacon. We do it.'

Deacon pointed. 'Look at them, colonel.'

'I look. I look to you too.'

135

The tinsel had stopped dancing before Deacon's eyes. His hearing was fine now. He felt stupid, standing there on the edge of so much carnage, with a German armoured column hastening towards him while he petulantly argued the toss with this fat little Russian. Stupid but also rather ashamed.

'What do you mean?' Deacon said.

'Last plan.'

'Ah!'

'I get wounded out, sledges. Ten minutes, quarter hour. All can go.'

'Yes, I agree.'

'Nina, your sergeant, stay.'

'Now hold on—'

'Twenty.' Safaryan held up his hands with the fingers spread. 'Twenty soldiers, one hundred my people. All guns. All shells. Nina, your sergeant.'

'And?'

'You, me, two more. We go?'

'Go? Go where?'

Safaryan turned to his right, away from the wrecked gate. He flung back the coat again, freeing his arm and shoulder, and pointed upward. 'Up there.'

'What in God's name for?'

'Blow top off mountain,' Boris Safaryan said.

6 Angels of death

Heavy grey clouds swept in from the west on the rising wind. Just as the retreat of wounded began, flakes of snow streaked the valley and soon the peaks of the Caucasus were swallowed up in a sluggish blizzard. Toiling up the highway, the German armoured column was blotted out. The sledges and improvised litters of wounded from Baku-Ashran trudged down towards the Ganevis through the falling snow, also to be lost to sight.

This was how Buz Campbell had always imagined Russia and he was heartened by a turn in the weather which he at first regarded as favourable. It did not occur to him that what was good for the guardians of the pass would be bad for Deacon's climbing team or that the colonel's bid to close the pass might be scuppered by the snowfall. Nina's anxiety brought the truth home to Buz.

Until that happened Buz had been pleased with developments, relieved to have his wounded pals on the way to safety, and happy enough to sit in a snow burrow, protected by camouflage sheets and jagged timbers, with a whopping great pile of ammunition packed into the hole behind him. Under the shell he showed to the world, Buz was still enough of a romantic to appreciate a heroic situation. Though he doubted if Operation Snowshoe would ever earn itself more than passing mention in the regiment's history, he was conscious that circumstances had made him the man on the spot, a role that all SAS-trained soldiers hankered after, one way or another.

The cold was less intense after the snow began.

In thick felt overboots and lined ski-suit, Buz was comfortable. He had eaten the canned meat that Nina had brought and drunk a little of the wine that one of the other girls had produced. He was glad to be shot of responsibility for the wounded, to see Deacon and P.B. set off, to be alone in the burrow with the Vaughan shotgun and the Vickers anti-tank gun and a working Bren.

All he really needed to make it all perfect was Nina.

He wanted her now, wanted her badly. He wanted to take her right there in the snow hole, with the wind beating madly at the canvas and the muffled roar of kraut tanks shuddering through the blank air. He wanted to taste her breasts and bury his face in her hair and lock her in his thighs. It was a crazy sexual yearning, linked with fighting and dying, an animal instinct, as if the ordeal they must undergo was a courtship rite.

Nina appeared suddenly through the curtain of snow. She dropped into the snow burrow by his side. Her cheeks were fiery with the flaying of the wind, her eyes bright. They spoke like soldiers, experts in warfare. Buz felt very close to Nina Safaryan at that moment, closer than he had ever done to anyone before.

'A quarter of an hour, the Germans will be within range,' she said. 'You will hear our mortars from the flanks.'

'How many?'

'Four emplacements; one mortar to each. Four men to each. Two to left, two to right of the highway.'

'Size?'

'The three-inch, of course.'

'HE ten-pounders? The ones from the Whitley?'

'Yes. We have so little number of bombs, though. Restricted to two rounds each minute, we can last for a quarter hour only.'

'Yeah, but that's all it'll take,' said Buz. 'The krauts are inside fifteen hundred yards already.'

'We start at low elevation, at one thousand yards. The snow does not matter to us. We must hold to the crest until Boris returns, then we must get all out, cross the river, over side of the mountain, to gobble the Germans up.'

'If there's enough of us for a blood hunt.'

'No mercy. No prisoners.'

'Right,' Buz said.

'What have you here?'

'Shotgun and three rifles. One Bren, bipod mounted. And the big baby, of course,' said Buz. 'It's the big baby we're counting on.'

Nina did not raise her eyes from his face to the shrouded two-pounder AT gun which Buz, with help, had bedded on its outriggers to the right of the emplacement, protected by the remains of the timber gate which stuck up, like rotten teeth, from a packed snow wall.

Time had been against them, time and manpower. The horses had struggled with the panniers of yellow-banded shells, 'fixed' APs. Though two hundred rounds had been listed as cargo for the paradrop, only eighty had reached Baku-Ashran.

'We work it together,' Buz said. 'I'll take the gunner's seat and you do your number as commander. You know how?'

'Yes.' She put her hand out on to his shoulder. 'We will be the prime target when it begins.'

'What's behind us?'

'The girls. My girls who are left.'

'And the partisans?'

'In trenches. Victor is in command.'

'What if Boris and Deacon don't make it?'

'We retreat only when we have to,' she said.

'I figured as much.'

'Snow is no good for climbers.'

'What's that supposed to mean?'

'No good for us.'

'You didn't answer my question.'

She smiled, her wide mouth sexy as hell. 'I have no answer.'

Buz wiped snow from his face. 'Give me one of those cigarettes. We've got time for that, ain't we?'

'Sadly, cigarettes is all we do have time for.'

She took out a case, gunmetal grey and polished with use, extracted two cigarettes, lit them with her petrol lighter and handed one to Buz. They were, hemmed in now by the veils of snow that draped the valley of the Dzera, Roshtan and the Tigers.

'How about later?' Buz said.

'We have time for everything,' she said.

There was nothing to stop him; he had her promise. He knew she wouldn't lie. Nothing to stop him having her – except twenty Pzkpfw IVs, three hundred panzer grenadiers and Christ knows how many Gebirgsjäger. And maybe, if the skies cleared, another formation of dive-bombers to contend with, or fifty loaded para-transports, or fuckin' Himmler himself winging down to shit on their heads.

Any other time, in any other place, he would have gotten his priorities right. Angry at the waste of opportunity, his rage extended outwards towards the krauts.

No mercy. No prisoners.

He sucked on the pungent cigarette.

The first smothered bark of mortar fire made him grin. 'Yeah!'

The woman got to her feet, stooped and kissed him on the mouth.

'Fight well, Buz Campbell,' she said.

'You too, kid,' he answered, and ran along the slanted burrow to strip the cover from the Vickers.

Jeff Deacon believed that he had come close to failing as a commander in the field. He had almost lost his nerve. He had allowed fear to overcome him and had very nearly cracked up. The unexpected appearance of the bombers had been the last straw. His relief at being given a chance to redeem himself was considerable. Grateful to Boris Safaryan, he was consequently more confident in the value of the plan than he might otherwise have been.

Even the sudden onset of the blizzard didn't draw Deacon back into despair. Safaryan gave no sign that the wind and snow presented any special hazards and Deacon drove on energetically, plunging his snow poles into the gully bed, trailing the figure of the girl thirty feet ahead of him.

What was her name – they all looked more or less alike to him – Natasha?

According to P.B., the girl was nothing but a trained monkey. P.B. said she reminded him of his wee sister Betty, only Betty was better-looking and couldn't ski. Deacon doubted if it was fraternal affection that made P.B. so attentive to the little

140

athlete. Certainly the girl showed no signs of flagging, even though she was burdened with a rucksack full of plastic explosive, weighing around eighty pounds, a Russian Sting slung across her chest.

Deacon's own load was lighter, the ropes, pitons and kara-biners needed for the traverse of a vertical rock face and the ascent of the four-pitch route which would lead him to the overhang. Wrapped about his waist was the coil of wire that he must feed from the charges to the detonator. Apart from his service revolver in its side holster, he had no weapon. It was hardly likely that they would encounter Germans two and a half thousand feet above the pass. On the steep face of Sokhara there was nothing but ice-plastered rock, no through route for men or machines.

Thank God wily Boris Safaryan had been alert.

Boris had set up this 'last ditch defence' a month ago. It had taken a dozen of the toughest mountaineers in the area ten hours to reach the summit ridge of Sokhara where they had spent a very cold night. Originally Boris had hoped to set charges in advance but he had been unable to lay hands on suitable explosives and impact fuses. Anything more random would not shake the mountain face with sufficient force to fissure the rock and cause the massive slide that Boris calculated would be needed to seal the pass below.

Lowered from the summit on abseil ropes, Boris's moun-taineers had drilled out and marked with blue dye holes into which explosive could later be placed. Much explosive would be needed to ensure success, though the north-west face of Sokhara was notoriously unstable. Just how dangerous a hazard to travellers through the pass the great bulging wall really was, would be proved soon enough.

Colonel Safaryan had hoped to check the German thrust with his private army, using only conventional weapons. He might have done so too, if it had not been for the big wind and, later, the intervention of the Luftwaffe. As soon as Safa-ryan heard the scream of the Stukas he knew that Deacon and he – or someone – would have to climb the north-west wall of Sokhara, plant explosive, and trust to luck on the result.

It took two hours of hard climbing to reach the waist of the gully, at which point the snow slope became too steep for skis. Sheltered from the worst of the wind which scraped across the vertical walls to their left, the four climbers stopped long enough to unclip their rods and strap crampons to their boots. Awkwardly latched to the back of the heavy rucksacks, the skis now became an added burden.

P.B., Deacon noticed, managed to light a cigarette during the pause and shared it with the Russian girl who, athlete or not, seemed to appreciate the taste of Virginia tobacco.

Safaryan pointed. 'See, Jeff. Three hundred feet. We climb. A shelf, you see.'

A coxcomb of snow spilled into the gully from the left wall at the point where the gully narrowed and steepened once more. The snow comb would probably be soft and treacherous. Deacon would take the lead here and navigate around the ledge – very long, Safaryan had told him – to the base of the wall. Wind and snow added to the difficulty, but conditions were no worse than Deacon had encountered in Scotland on several occasions in the past. Spiked in the snow, the skis would be left at the bottom of the comb.

The party moved up the constricted gully, Safaryan in the lead. Cutting no steps but kicking in crampon points, the colonel held himself close against the snow to retain balance, the weight of the pack dragging on him. For such a rotund little man, Safaryan was incredibly graceful, Deacon thought. He had that poise and rhythm which is an attribute of all skilled mountaineers.

Natasha and McNair were nimble too.

Bringing up the rear, Deacon felt himself clumsy by comparison. He put his head down and concentrated on following the dents that the leader's crampons had made in the hardening snow.

In an odd sort of way Deacon was looking forward to the climb, to getting to grip, at last, with a problem as tangible and as simple as a rock wall.

142

The night had been cold enough to cement the rocks and loose pockets of snow, and the temperature rise, with the advent of the blizzard, had unlocked only the surface skin. Only thin rivulets of icy dust and an occasional pebble hissed and chuckled down the drainpipe gully.

Safaryan reached the base of the coxcomb. Deacon now saw that it was composed of an arched rib of broken rock behind which snow had built up in caked layers. The colonel unstrapped an ice-pick, much shorter in the shaft than the type to which Deacon was accustomed, and offered it to the captain.

'Nothing longer?'

'It all I have.'

Deacon breathed through his mouth, calming himself. He craned his neck and studied the first problem.

'I'll climb the rib, not the snow.'

Safaryan expressed no surprise.

'Two ropes?' the colonel said.

'Should do it,' said Deacon. 'I'll bring up P.B. next and he can haul up the sacks on slings. Then the young lady. You come last, colonel, if you will. Once P.B. is on the ledge, I'll forge ahead and recce the wall.'

'Sure, sure.'

Deacon shed the sack. He could still feel its weight for a moment, pressing him forward like a phantom fist in the small of the back. He dug two lengths of rope from the rucksack; quality hemp, unused and hairy, the ends neatly sealed with black tape. He knotted the ropes about him. Hemp would collect quite a lot of snow dust and would increase the drag as he climbed. But the run-out wouldn't be more than a couple of hundred feet, assuming he could find a stance close to the top of the rib where the ledge started. He would want a very solid belay from which to sling the karibiner. The haul would be in the region of eighty pounds per sack, plus a fall factor in case the girl or the colonel slipped. P.B. would be fine as a second. He had been thoroughly schooled in mountaincraft and was quite at home with ropes, snap-links and slings.

Deacon removed his crampons and put them, points inward, into the rucksack, strapped it up securely, then, without removing his gloves, stepped in close against the rock and studied it for a full minute.

P.B. lit another cigarette.

Deacon took a deep breath, and reached for his first hand-hold, a nice, solid jughandle. He drew up, placed the stiffened toe of his boot on a knob and pushed. Climbing with his legs as he had been taught to do, he used the strong muscles of thighs and calves, not fingers and forearms. He would need all his strength for the work ahead. No sense in burning himself out on the first pitch of the day.

The rib was a piece of cake. Come to think of it, it *looked* like cake, wedding cake, black and rich, topped with brittle icing sugar.

Once he had attained a height of thirty feet, the remainder was little more than a cautious scramble. It took Deacon five minutes to complete the pitch.

Carefully he stepped on to the quilt of snow that draped the nether edge of the ledge. More of a little terrace, really, Deacon thought, broad enough to furnish an Alpinist with a very comfortable bivouac. He unslung the lengths of hemp from around his shoulder and picked out a strong snap-link; a modern job, probably German. He prised it open, inserted the rope, closed the karibiner and fed a double length of sling and the climbing rope through it then searched behind him on the gable for a suitable belay. He found a peach – an oval stone wedged into a fissure directly behind a spike. Swiftly he tied on. He snapped the climbing rope free and rolled a couple of loops down it, like a circus cowboy, and called to P.B. that he was ready.

Seconds later the Scotsman shouted, 'Right?'

'Come awa', laddie,' Deacon cried and gave the rope a tiny, mischievous tweak.

Minutes later, P.B.'s hood appeared by the coxcomb, shoulders following. He was well into the swing of it, palm supported on the snow, climbing neatly up the spine of rock. To Deacon he resembled a sword-dancer, so quick and precise were his movements.

P.B. joined the captain on the terrace. He took over the belay and, on a separate safety rope, began the laborious business of hand-hauling the rucksacks, a process that could not be hurried for fear of damaging the plastic explosive and fuses.

'How many snap-links do you have, P.B.?'

'Four.'

'Hook the sacks on to the belay point to keep them safe.'

'Right.'

'I'll toddle round the corner.'

'Watch it.'

'Have no fear,' said Deacon.

Deacon would have felt a little more secure if he had had his favourite long-shaft ice axe with him, though its benefits would have been largely psychological; there were no steps to cut, not enough stable snow for them anyhow. The captain edged round the buttress with considerable caution.

Directly beneath him the valley opened out. Though screened by snow and billowing cloud, it gave Deacon a sense of extreme exposure after the confined gully. He could feel the tug of space, that first flinching to which he soon adjusted and almost began to enjoy, a soaring sensation, free and stimulating. He wondered how the girl would take to it; he assumed that the Safaryans had selected one who had had climbing experience.

Deacon picked his way along the dwindling terrace, along steepening eaves of snow. Here ice had infiltrated the rock plates and made them slippery.

The wind tugged and snapped at his clothing, swirled falling snow into horizontal patterns that further blotted out his bird's-eye view of the valley and, more particularly, of the pass. He calculated that he must be over Baku-Ashran, somewhere above the sugarloaf-shaped corner that the timber half-gate had been built on to. Perhaps not quite so far as that yet. Over the stretch where the long tents had been pitched, on the Ganevis side of the summit? Hard to tell exactly. He listened, imagining he could hear gunfire. He could not be sure, though, that it wasn't some acoustical trick of the wind.

In clear weather would he have been visible to German telescopes? Would the jerries have had the savvy to scout the peaks so high above the pass? The points were absolutely moot. There was no sign of a break in the cloud roof, or of the snow abating.

The terrace smeared out into a rock wall.

Rock reared above Deacon and plunged down into cloud.

Without doubt, this was the commencement of the traverse that Safaryan had described.

Deacon worked his way forward into the corner where snow had sculpted a huge organ-pipe topped by a knobbly crown of water ice. He boot-hacked a stance in the snow and rummaged about in search of reliable belays. He found two stout spikes, no chocks.

The corner was studded with edgy little holds dusted with fresh snow but not, thank God, varnished with ice. Deacon's boots were shod with Vibram, part of a consignment that Holms had filched from an Italian convoy. He was uncertain how much grip the cleated rubber would afford on Verglas. He hated Verglas, that thin, almost invisible, coating of ice that one often found in the Alps after a night's hoar frost. On the other hand, if there was no Verglas then the route might be very loose. According to Safaryan, the north-west face of Sokhara was a gigantic heap of slag, a geological freak in this region of granite massifs and eroded limestone peaks.

What the devil does it matter, Deacon told himself. The damned thing has to be climbed, even if I have to do it barefoot or in stocking-soles.

The realization that this was no mere weekend jaunt in the Tyrol tweaked Deacon's nerves. Venturing to the edge of the corner, he examined the rock more closely. With the wind hard in his face, he peered across the wall to a handsome ledge, all of sixty yards long and about as broad as a railway platform. Dear God, he could have drilled a platoon on it – if, that is, he could have persuaded a platoon to follow him across a vertical face, a couple of hundred feet of decidedly tricky climbing, to reach it.

The wind and the streaking snow would, without doubt, make life a little harder. But the climb itself did not appear to be awfully difficult, in spite of its exposure.

Deacon returned to the corner and impatiently awaited the arrival of the rest of the party.

At length, P.B. appeared, weighted down by two rucksacks attached to the rope which snaked out behind him. The girl followed, dragging another two rucksacks along the sloping terrace. The colonel brought up the rear.

With a hundred and twenty pounds of plastic explosive on his back, even P.B. had to struggle and his progress across the terrace was slow. Deacon moved to help the little Scot but P.B. waved him away, lumbering on to the corner where, with Deacon's aid, he unslung the sacks and hooked them on to the belay spike that Deacon had cleared for the purpose.

Egged on by Safaryan, Deacon wasted no time in tying himself to the climbing rope and, with P.B. as second, tackled the traverse.

He kept the line to the big ledge as straight as possible and, along the route, placed two slings and karibiners on natural belays. Two more runners were on hammered pitons, the thick metal nails that climbers used, a bunch of which jangled like keys on a waistloop at Deacon's thigh. As there would be no need to retrieve the pitons, Deacon banged them in to the heads.

Strung out on the hitched ropes, a run of two hundred feet, the captain picked his way across the breast of the rock wall, keeping a wary eye out for icy patches and sections of crumbly rock. He could understand now why Safaryan had taken his advance party on to the north-west face by way of abseil ropes from the summit. The traverse was not the sort of place that one wanted to play about on. It demanded sureness, confidence and expert technique.

When Deacon attained the broad ledge, he found to his disappointment that, though large, it was raked at an uncomfortable angle and that he could not completely relax upon it.

He belayed and brought P.B. to him.

Unburdened, the Scots climbed quickly across to Deacon and together the SAS men ferried in the rucksacks on an improvised pulley, using every inch of two one-fifty lengths of rope that they had with them.

In cold climates, plastic explosive was usually very stable and could be manhandled without danger of detonation. Even so, the weight and shape of the sacks required caution and Deacon was relieved when all four loads were securely tucked against the inner wall of the ledge, fastened to pitons.

The girl ate up the traverse, moving without hesitation across the face, totally unconcerned that beneath her lay eight or nine hundred feet of fresh air. She looked quite beautiful, Deacon thought, with her hood down and her keen, pert little face exposed, wind ruffling her short, black hair.

Safaryan came last.

Unsure, nervous and, for once, robbed of bouncy confidence, the colonel clung to the rock, stabbing his feet, screwed up by fear of the long, long drop. Kneeling, Deacon encouraged the Russian, cajoling him to ease tensed muscles and swing more freely from position to position. Will-power alone could not oil the colonel's locked joints, however. As a skier of considerable ability, he had no fear of heights. But the traverse was something different, a new variation, and Deacon knew only too well that clenching vertigo could overcome anyone, even seasoned rock climbers.

Safaryan lurched, stretched, grasped at the ledge. Deacon grabbed his forearms and yanked him, kicking, on to the ramp.

Safaryan forced a sickly, white-faced grin.

'I – I expose myself, no?'

'I wouldn't, if I were you,' said Deacon. 'You could lose more than your dignity.'

Panting, the Russian lay belly on the snow for almost a minute before he drew up his knees and, spooked now, crawled along the inside of the ledge.

'Is he gonna freeze on us?' P.B. hissed.

'I hope not,' said Deacon.

'He's no' climbin', is he? On the wall, I mean.'

'Of course not,' said Deacon. 'But he'll have to show us where the charges are to be placed and help the girl with the ropes.'

As if he had overheard, Boris Safaryan forced himself to stand upright and take his hands from reassuring holds on the rock. He tried to appear relaxed but swayed, bent forward and teetered against the steep angle.

'I okay! Okay! Sure, sure! Okay now!' he shouted.

The girl glanced at Deacon, awaiting his command.

In dumb show, Deacon told her to unpack the rucksacks and lay out the ingots of plastic explosive. While she did so, Deacon put on his gloves and walked along the length of the ledge, past Safaryan.

Fortunately, the dye marks were easy to spot. Potent chemical colours, the stains had survived a month's storms and snowfalls, soaking out from naked rock through plastering snow to plot the positions that Safaryan's team had selected and prepared for the charges.

There was some sort of pattern discernible even from below, though Deacon could not see the upper level under its great caped overhang, only blocks of blackish rock jutting downwards like the gates of a portcullis. The overhang was incredibly imposing, a mirror image of the ledge on which he stood. In wisping cloud and flying snow, it looked as if the whole top of the mountain was perched on it. He began to realize that Safaryan's statement that they would blow the mountain up was no exaggeration after all.

Fumbling in his pocket, Deacon found a bar of broken chocolate. He unwrapped it, licked it from the tinfoil into his mouth and chewed thoughtfully. Dabbing snow from the rock with his thumb, he sucked it. He needed energy, lots of energy.

Roughly estimated, he fancied he might be up there, like a damned spider spinning a web, for two or three hours. He hoped that Safaryan's Caucasians had had the sense to make the charge holes accessible. He counted four dye marks on the first level, forty feet up from the ledge and thirty to forty feet apart. A hundred or so feet above them, on a slabby, piebald sheet of rock, he could make out another couple of inky blue stains. Four more were strategically situated right under the overhang. He hoped to God he could reach them.

He helped himself to another dab of snow to get the bitter taste of chocolate out of his mouth.

Safaryan inched unsteadily towards him.

'You do it?' the colonel asked, panting slightly.

'I think so,' said Deacon. 'I won't know for sure until I get up there.'

'All ready! Plastic. Fuse. Wire. Go now, please.'

Deacon grinned and shook his arms, waggling his hands which, inside the gloves, had warmed up nicely. He felt loose again and not intimidated by the magnitude of the task before him.

'P.B.,' he shouted. 'Are you ready?'

'Waitin' for you, Jeff.'

'What do you think?' Deacon asked the colonel.

'Go to top first. Straight up.'

'I agree,' said Deacon. 'Run the wire through the alloy karibiners, splice it on to a vee lead and bring a single wire back to the detonator box.'

'Aye, but we canny carry all that stuff in one go,' P.B. put in.

'Can we?'

'We'll do the top level and the second, then come down for a rest and more explosive.'

'You're leadin'?'

'Oh, yes,' said Deacon.

He attached himself to the climbing rope and ran it free to P.B., then lifted the rucksack of plastic explosive which the girl had prepared. He slipped it against his body, straps around his back, wearing the sack against his chest.

Next he hung the pouch of copper charges around him and strapped it down with his waistloop upon which clinked an armoury of climbing hardware which weighed more, Deacon

150

felt, than the blessed rucksack itself. He was unused to hauling all this weight up rock-faces. He glanced over at P.B. who was similarly encumbered and also had the wire coil to contend with. It was not the sort of exercise that the SAS had ever rehearsed. He wondered what Paddy Gogarty and old Walter would have thought of it all.

Deacon stood to the wall and selected a line.

The wall was devoid of prominent features. But there was a crack of sorts straggling up towards the slab and, on the slab, an overlap edge that might yield friction.

Behind him to his right, Boris Safaryan tied himself on to the rock and, with a snort of determination, braced himself to hook on to the end of the two-man climbing rope. He faced outwards, eyes unblinking, round features compressed with the effort of keeping fear in check as he stared into the white sky.

Deacon took off his gloves and dropped them on to the ledge at his feet. He wore woollen mittens, fingerless but long, to keep some warmth in his wrists and forearms.

Canting side-on to the rock, he executed the first lift. Looking down at his positioning, he reached up his right arm, found a hold and leaned back on it. The rucksack sagged away from his chest. He should have worn the rucksack properly but he could not depend upon finding a suitable stance up top, one big enough to allow him to make the delicate manoeuvre of transfer. As it was, he could hang and work with some degree of comfort.

Below him, Safaryan spoke with the girl in Russian. She tied herself on to the rope too, an extra precaution in case Deacon fell.

Pursing his lips, Deacon soundlessly whistled a BBC *Radio Dancehall* tune and climbed more or less in rhythm to its banal tempo.

One *and* two.

And one and two.

The sequence of holds on the lower face came easily to him. But he did not charge it and tested each hold before he put weight on it. Sokhara was, after all, a slag heap.

The snow was loose and dry and not particularly bothersome. If he had been forced to climb by friction holds, the little sloped plates one found on some of the modern routes in Wales, for instance, he would have been in trouble. But the north-west wall was plentifully supplied with cracks, rib-edges and square-shaped knuckle-sized blocks. Deacon made the first eighty feet, past the lowest level of blue-dye stains, without having to pause.

Reaching, balancing, reaching and bracing, using a combination of leg and arm, he planted his first peg at eighty feet. The piton rang in and, when he tested it, gave no sign of shake. He clipped on, ran the rope through and shouted to P.B. to come after him, then, trusting the Scot, carried on upward.

At the base of the slab – a huge sheet of fissured stone buckled by eons of pressure from above and set at the slant of a bungalow roof – Deacon found a stance that enabled him to bring up P.B.

The Scots corporal was perfectly relaxed. Standing one below the other, the couple surveyed the remainder of the route. Now they could see the overhang and the upper dye marks, four large blots upon the vertical section directly beneath the rock portcullis.

'Will plastic be enough t'bring that lot down?'

'We won't know until we try,' said Deacon. 'Safaryan seems to think it will. There's thousands of tons of rock perched on the overhang, P.B. Any sort of blasting is bound to disturb the strata. I wouldn't be surprised if we do manage to bring the house down.'

'Christ!' said P.B., awed.

'How are you?'

'Fingers're numb, that's all.'

'Put your gloves on then, and give me secure protection. I'm going directly up the slab's edge to the overhang. When I reach the first of the marks I'll fix a peg runner before I traverse left. I'll be in sight all the way, P.B.'

The Scot said, 'Can you manage wi' all that gear?'

'Of course.'

'An' the wire?'

'It sounds more difficult and complicated than it is,' said Deacon. 'I'll probably be able to run a straight wire through my own pegs, you see, linked on to the copper charges.'

'Aye,' said P.B., dubiously.

When the corporal was ready to attend the protective rope, Deacon climbed on.

He found the slab edge awkward, though there was no scarcity of holds. Heavily burdened and unbalanced, he wondered if he would have been more prudent to bring up the sacks after he had found a stance at the upper level. Time, however, was against him. He had not forgotten Buz and the Russians gathered at the summit of the pass or the fact that the Germans would be advancing doggedly and that this morning there would be no retreat.

When he reached the first of the dye stains, under the looming roof of rock, Deacon drove in a piton, clipped a karibiner to it, threaded through the climbing rope and struck left across the upper rim of the slab.

The climbing here was delicate; little, fragile holds for his toes, nothing for the whole hand, only sharp edges for his fingertips, almost too sharp. The upper face had a brittle feel to it. The snow, oddly, was moist, not dry, as if the protected part of the face had absorbed the warmth of yesterday's sunlight in defiance of the cold night airs. The wind too was rather a problem. It hurtled round the prow of the mountain in staggering gusts. Deacon had to be constantly on his guard, steady and secure at all times, prepared to brace against the blasts.

As he passed each of the dye stains, he inspected the cracks that the Russian team had selected to receive the plastic. One crack had been widened with a chisel and had filled up with snow which he scooped out with his fingers. The cracks were all deep and would pack nicely with the pliable explosive.

Engrossed in his task now, Deacon was unaware of the vast grey space that yawned at his heels – a thousand feet of free-fall to the tumbling snows that capped the rocks above the narrowest part of the pass. It was effort, not fear, that caused him to perspire and pant as he fumbled open the rucksack on his chest and, balanced by the first of the cracks, took out a soft grey-yellow brick of the army's latest top-quality explosive.

Deacon had set more than his share of charges but he was no technician, really. He had no idea what this stuff was composed of or what crowd of War Office boffins had developed it. He assumed that it contained a quantity of nitro-glycerine stabilized in a 'secret' base of cellulose compound. He had been informed that the substance was to be treated like ordinary explosive but that on electrical detonation the shock front would be violent and exceedingly steep. The new substance had the advantage of being more potent, ounce for ounce, than dynamite or any of the plastics that had so far been issued to the SAS, and only a low electrical charge was required to detonate it. God knows, the charge box was small enough, hardly bigger than a tea-caddy.

Standing erect, Deacon took the brick in his right hand and crammed it into the crack, pressing and moulding it gently until only a fist-sized patch remained visible. He fixed the prongs of the copper lead to it, tapped the plate with his knuckles and threaded and knotted the stout copper wire into the eyelets on the plate. He gave the device a tentative tug, found it all firm and snug and, spooling out the wire as he went, worked his way back to the second of the preselected cracks.

It took him thirty minutes to rig the upper level's four charges and lead the wire back down to P.B.'s stance.

By then Deacon's calves were beginning to feel the strain, to tremble slightly when he paused on scant holds. His back too had begun to ache in protest against the sagging weight of the rucksack. He knew that he should rope off the wall and rest for fifteen or twenty minutes on the ledge below. But Deacon was not inclined to be sensible. He still felt guilty at what had happened in Roshtan and, only hours ago, at the half-gate. Flogging his body was some kind of penance. Without compunction, he drove himself across the vast broken plane of the slab.

Deacon had been on the wall now for over an hour. He

knew that he was tiring because he no longer sweated and felt the chill of the wind on the surface of the skin of his body. His hands had lost all feeling and it was difficult to perform the small manipulations required with the charge plates, leads and wire. P.B. had offered to plant the two charges on the slab but this was Jeff Deacon's show and the captain would have none of it.

The climb across the slab was excessively severe.

Mercifully there were only two charges to be placed there, a couple of bricks of malleable plastic stuffed into deep holes, like miniature caverns; almost arm's-length deep, in fact. Above him he could see the copper wire. Very neatly strung, though he said so himself.

Rock crumbled like stale fruit-cake. The edges of holds broke. The snow here seemed fine and infiltrative. Deacon's fingers felt like pork sausages. The drag of the sack pained his chest and belly muscles. He detached his mind from physical discomfort and bore down again, concentrating on each movement, keeping it easy, keeping tension at bay. The hammer, though, seemed to have grown monstrously heavy. It waggled as he banged in pitons. The snap-links were stiff and, in spite of himself, he cursed them obscenely as he struggled to prise open their jaws. He should have brought Buz instead of P.B. Dear God, if he peeled off in this position, P.B. would be far too slight to hold him.

He envisaged pitons popping out like press-studs, saw himself scraped across the slab like a puppet on a broken string; then falling, falling and falling, down past the Russians, down and down to the crown of the sugarloaf, splashing bloodily over it, flensed like a side of beef, to land at Buz Campbell's feet.

'Hey, Deke; you okay?'

'Absolutely.'

'You got troubles?'

'No. Now shut up.'

P.B. said no more.

It took Deacon fifteen minutes to cross the slab to the further dye mark, twenty to fill and set the charge.

His hands had almost ceased to be connected to his brain. Was this what frost-bite felt like? He stuck his fingertips into his mouth but that did not one damned bit of good. Disgustedly he spat out flecks of wool from the palm mittens.

The wire seemed to coil like a snake, like something with a mind of its own. He was becoming very, very tense now. Too cold, too sore to detach mind from body any more.

He fed copper wire through the snap-link on its piton and rested as best he could, brow against the slab, eyes closed.

'Hey, Jeff—?'

'Shut up, wee man,' Deacon murmured.

'Hear it?' P.B. called.

Opening his eyes, lifting his head, Deacon stared upwards at the slab, beyond it to the rock eaves of the overhang. He could hardly believe that he had been up there, worked there.

What *was* that sound? Had the mountain decided to retaliate, to blow its top without assistance?

'Guns,' P.B. informed him. 'Hear them? Mortars.'

'Ah, yes,' said Deacon.

He stole a moment to listen.

Gusts of wind and thickening snow dissipated the sounds, diffused them. But he thought that he could separate from the growling the *pah-pah*, *pah-pah* reports of British-made mortars.

He smiled, nodding. Giving them hell? Yes, the partisans would be giving them hell. The cantata grew fainter, *pianissimo*. Then it came back with sudden staccato, double *forte*. The Vickers AT gun. It sounded again. Buz and the blonde Russian were working well. He discerned other noises. Tanks, no doubt.

'Shake a fuckin' leg, Jeff.'

'What? Yes, of course.'

Deacon pulled himself together.

The import of the racket from the valley far, far below, stirred his exhaustion. The Tigers must be within a thousand yards of Baku-Ashran, rumbling on towards the gun emplacements on the summit of the high road. Over the rock step. Rumbling, rumbling on.

From below, Safaryan was shouting at him.

156

Even the little Russian girl was chirping excitedly, like a damned myna bird.

Deacon swung his right leg, took a pinch hold on a little friable block with swollen fingertips, swung his pelvis and, like a pregnant kangaroo, lurched sideways. Did the same thing again, swinging into a clumsy dance step, a hop. He really was very tired, very leaden, beaten.

The sounds of battle were constant.

Safaryan was still shouting.

Deacon saw the shark's-fin hold out of the corner of his eye. He swung the leg again, gripped the fin with both hands and pendulumed to his right.

The rock fin snapped and broke cleanly away from the slab.

Deacon fell.

When planted on its retractable outriggers, the Vickers-Armstrong high-velocity anti-tank cannon had a traverse of 360° and an elevation of minus 13° to plus 15°. Its muzzle velocity was 2,616 feet per second. The projectiles weighed a tidy 2 pounds, 6 ounces each, and the gun could pump out 22 rounds of fixed, AP ammunition per minute.

Seated left of the muzzle, behind an armour-plated shield, the gunner controlled elevation by means of a vertical hand-wheel upon which was mounted the trigger. Traverse required manipulation of a second handwheel to the right of the gunner's seat. For rapid traverse of pedestal, gunner and gun, a throw-out clutch could be released by foot-pedal and the whole unit spun by the action of the gun commander pressing upon the gunner's shoulders.

Three independent sights provided refinement in gauging range and line, from 1,200 to 1,500 yards after initial setting and on 100-yard increments thereafter. The effective destructive range was, however, a mere 500 yards.

According to the handbook, Vickers two-pounders should be towed into position by ¾ ton trucks. Buz noted that portage could also be undertaken by two large horses assisted by twelve demented Russian peasants, and decided that he might mention this in a letter to compilers of TN 30–410 for inclusion in the manual's next revised edition.

Maybe he would also report that the cannon could be operated pretty well by a man and a woman, working without expertise but driven by the sort of desperation that is occasioned by the sight of a column of twenty German Tigers snorting towards you.

Ammo was in short supply. At least two panniers of shells had gone missing after the wayward drop. In fact Safaryan's search parties had been goddamned lucky to find the gun still roped to its delivery sled and undamaged, though its two 'chutes had both torn off and were nowhere to be found.

There was no question of blasting away at the Germans. Buz selected targets with care, fiddled with the scope and horizontal line finder, dickered with the elevation, crossed his fingers, signalled to Nina to get down and cover her ears, then touched the trigger.

The first shell surprised him. He hadn't noticed the tracer code on it when he had rammed it into the breech.

White lightning arched towards the lead tank and struck it on the turret with a raucous explosion. More by luck than judgement, he had gotten range and elevation just right. There wasn't too much recoil, only a sort of start that ran through all the gun's parts, and the stink of black powder or whatever it was, and the plume of smoke that flowed out of the apertures on top of the breech block.

Buz touched nothing.

He fired a second shell.

The din in the burrow was enough to squeeze your brains out of your ears. What the hell must it be like to be tending a 25-pounder, one of the field howitzers that the Royal Artillery cursed blue-blind? The thought was whisked away by the shell's explosion and the effect of his targetry on the Tiger.

Shrieking with delight, Nina was prancing about behind him like a Cossack dancer.

He couldn't blame her. The first tank was a gonner, smashed like a goddamned Woolworth alarm clock. Smoke poured from

158

the body, obscuring the vehicle's erratic course and eventual nosedive over the edge of the highway. It did not fall far, only twenty feet or so, but it was obviously out of the game for good and all.

The partisans' mortars continued to pound the kraut column.

The second Tiger opened up now, flinging shells with amazing rapidity over the burrow. Sheets of debris poured backwards on to the canvas screens and camouflage hood above the Canadian's head.

'Keep the same range,' Nina howled.

Buz pressed the trigger.

The third missile ploughed along the plate that guarded the tank's tracks. He saw the tank deviate then straighten, and knew that the off-centre shot had made no impression on its heavy armour.

First time had just been luck, he guessed.

Still, five hundred yards off, the Tiger column had slowed. Maybe the accuracy of the side-hill mortars was telling. Maybe the panzer leader was just being cautious, protecting his limited manpower. Christ knows! Buz didn't reckon that the tanks' long-guns could get at them yet, not without finagling the pitch of the shots – which must be friggin' hard to do when you're crawling under fire.

Behind the emplacement by the remnants of the timber gate, though, the trenches must be taking a pasting. If he had been in charge back there, maybe he would have cleared them out, spread the lines.

The lead tank was down to less than walking pace, hardly progressing at all. He couldn't work out why. It was Nina who shouted the answer to his unspoken question.

'They tighten the column. Stragglers come in.'

'Yeah, sure, that's it,' Buz cried over his shoulder.

'Shoot, shoot.'

He clicked the knob above the horizontal line sight, squinted through it, and crossed the Tiger's turret.

Fired.

Again the shell struck at a withering angle. It did not explode

159

exactly on contact but burst somewhere behind the metal monster. He could not hear the screams of the wounded grenadiers but he saw them squirming out on to the banked snow at the highway's verge.

The Tiger's hull MG blazed, and above Buz the snow canvas was whopped by a stream of bullets.

Nina flung herself down behind the gun's left outrigger.

Fortunately the Tiger lurched, sinking into softer snow, and the hail of bullets chattered away overhead into the snow-streaked sky.

Nina pulled herself up beside Buz.

The Canadian didn't need to be told.

Fired.

The shell exploded against the turret at hull level. Whether this was the Tiger's weak spot or not, Buz couldn't be sure, but it did enough immediate damage to bring the brute to a standstill.

'More, more, more,' the woman shouted.

Fired.

A clear miss.

Jesus! how could that happen? He hadn't touched anything, hadn't tampered with a wheel or a whisker, hadn't even inhaled. And the friggin' shell was off-target! Maybe the tank had slouched. Jesus!

He was concentrating so much on the Tiger that he didn't hear the shell-burst back down the highway, didn't remark the column of frozen snow and red earth that it hurled upwards.

Buz was beginning to lose confidence in his skill as a gunner.

When he peered through the sighting slot, however, he saw that the lead tank had halted completely and that the rest of the column, as much of it as he could make out in the fuzzy grey light, had washed up against it, hugged in back of its hull.

At least the goddamned MG had quit firing.

He hardly noticed the shots let off by the grenadiers. Flea-bites. Chickenshit little pop-guns.

'Buz.' Nina sank her fingers into his neck, twisting his head. Round the rim of the shield he saw it.

One friggin' big kraut tank larruping up at full belt out of the valley. A wall of snow came with it, flattened as the tank hoisted over the verge of the highway and, travelling some, headed at them from ten-thirty on the left flank.

You stupid lame-brain, he cried silently, dismayed at his ineptness and ignorance. He should have realized that the column had gotten far enough up the track to use the skirt shoulder, broadened in the construction of the highway, to run tanks through out of sight of his position.

The first shell from the long-gun went past, close enough to burn the hair in his goddamned nostrils. The explosion almost collapsed his ear-drums.

Two more shells in rapid succession brought the rock shoulder behind him outwards in a spray of debris, pouring down to rip the screens away and fill the far end of the burrow. Nina had flattened herself on the snow again and only the gun's armour-plate shield saved him from serious wounding. The rubbish whanged off, denting it, gnawing out holes in the rim. Chunks of rock hummed about his head.

'Roll me round, Nina! Jesus, woman! Roll me round!'

The Tiger was storming towards them, long-gun turned fifteen to twenty degrees off the line of its advance, trained right between his eyes, its MG spurting.

But the big blonde Russian wasn't all mouth and pussy.

She booted off the throw-clutch before Buz could even remember where it was, flung her arms around his neck, her weight fully on him and, driving with her thighs, got the whole unit to rotate.

She used too much force, though. Buz bawled at her to brake. She braked and thrust again, like a bargee on a lock gate, only it wasn't no spar of wood but his shoulders she was hauling on. The muzzle came round and he stabbed at the trigger and heard the voice of the Vickers and felt shock radiate back from the recoil chamber, and nearly lost his head as Nina jerked back and fell off the pedestal.

Neither of them saw the projectile, though its path was as clear as day, as it skidded straight up the Tiger's breast-plate and rammed itself under the lid. It exploded violently a split second after contact.

Tigers at one hundred yards, given luck, weren't immune to anti-tank guns after all, no matter what friggin' Adolf's propagandists led you to believe.

Neither Buz nor Nina ever figured out what caused the tank to burst into flames. Spare petrol tanks fitted externally, maybe. Whatever – the Tiger vanished in a swirl of shiny red fire, licked about by curls of black smoke like ostrich feathers.

'YEAH-HA!' Buz punched the air with his fist. 'YEAH-HA!'

But Buz's jubilation was short-lived.

The flame-enshrouded tank did not grind to a halt. It came crashing on, way to the left now, bearing down the length of the emplacement.

Nina flung herself once more on Buz's shoulders. The Vickers swivelled through an angle of 90°s. The barrel jarred on the snow wall. Buz snatched at the trigger. He saw the short flight of the shell, forty yards at most, and felt as if his head had been chopped off by the reverberation of the explosion.

The advancing Tiger blew up.

It didn't fly apart, though. It shuddered and lifted and then ploughed, snout down, as the weight of its cannon ripped the steel turret out by the roots.

Through the mass of flames and shimmering heat, a second Tiger, whole and undamaged, passed. Buz saw it faintly, like a spectre, like the soul passing out of the body of the burning hulk that had forged on a final ten yards to block the Vickers and their exit from the emplacement. No crew members struggled from the turret of the wrecked Tiger and Buz guessed that, at any moment, its cargo of shells might explode. Anyhow, the panzers now had a clearway to the summit, bypassing the emplacement. A partition of reeking smoke and flames isolated him.

Leaping from the gunner's seat, he grabbed Nina by the waist and pitched himself headlong into the trough of snow to the right, into pitted debris. He covered her body with his.

It wasn't the Tiger that blew, though. It was the Vickers.

Shell, grenade or mortar bomb, Buz had no idea what took the AT gun out. It just flew apart, barrel folding like a flower stalk, the shield, all in one piece, sailing over his head like a boomerang. Metal chunks embedded themselves in the snow inches from his shoulder and legs. The retractable outriggers snapped on their hinges and jerked the stump of the gun upwards like some grotesque insect about to alight on his back.

Below him, Nina was shouting, squirming her body deeper into the snow, an involuntary response to the hellish noise of whirring fragments.

Minutes after the Vickers took its hit, shrapnel still fell like rain about them. The small angry sounds were more terrifying than the roar of the burning tank, intimate harbingers of death. But even with head singing and eyes blinded by smoke, Buz was calculating, figuring.

When he got to his feet he wasted no time in explanations. He grabbed the woman under the armpits and hoisted her to her knees. Her eyes were squeezed shut and she was still shouting garbled Russian cuss-words, as close to the edge of hysteria as he could let her go. He pulled her all the way up and cuffed her, slack-handed, across the face, drawing the blow but making it sting. Her eyes clicked open and she gaped at him, fish-mouthed with astonishment, though whether at the slap or at the fact that she was still alive was more than Buz could tell.

Behind him the burning Tiger howled and crackled, singeing hair on the sergeant's neck.

The burrow looked like a goddamned junk-yard.

'Nina?'

'I – I—' She stammered in Russian.

'We've got to get out of here,' Buz yelled.

It was no longer a matter of holding the pass, of stopping the krauts, but of sheer survival.

Any second now the grenadiers would swarm over the snow wall, darting through the smoke and heat vapour. And there was that second tank, the mirage, which had gone sliding past. Where the fuck had it wound up, and how many others had followed in its wake?

Pushing Nina towards the back of the burrow, Buz turned and searched among the junk. He found the Vaughan half-buried in snow but undamaged, grabbed it and pushed Nina again, bulled her ahead of him through the torn canvas camouflage screen and out on to a corner of the highway that lay behind the gate.

There were two tanks through.

But they hadn't got far.

Buz had seen a lot of weird things when it came to men against tanks, but nothing like this before. The Tigers' hulls were covered in bodies; not corpses, the bodies of Russian peasants. Ant-like, they smothered the armour, hung from the muzzle of the long-gun, and clung to the track mantels, a black and ugly mass that seemed intent on devouring the vehicles.

Every villager left at Baku-Ashran was there, perched on or draped about the Tigers. Jesus, they were smothering the friggin' tanks to death, sandbagging them into immobility: fifty, sixty peasants, women and boys mostly, swarming all over, armed with clubs and staves, reaping hooks and bolases of barbed wire, a few with Stings and fewer still with grenades, and the surrounding crowd flinging up sacks to them.

He knew why the tanks had bogged down; the commanders were terrified. He would have been terrified too. It was like being attacked by rats, a rat pack of unthinkable size and ferocity. Every technique for destruction was being employed at once, while up on the shoulder of the mountain, just across the head of the chasm, armed partisans were bringing in the mortars.

Regrouping? The word was ridiculously inappropriate. They were running crazy with the armaments they had left. Maybe *he* had thought of flight, escape. Not the Caucasians. If the krauts wanted the highway beyond the pass, they would have to slaughter every peasant who ever was, and roll their battle tanks over a carpet of bloody corpses.

Skittering flurries of snow obscured precise detail. Buz couldn't fathom how the Russians had gotten the tanks to check in the first place. All tank commanders knew that the

164

best defence against infantry was to mow them down, use superior power and weight. Then Buz saw the wire, yards of it, rusty baling wire and barbed wire and soft, thick coils of cable, the dregs of every farmyard cellar and loft, scrapings from barns and stys, wire stripped from fences. Christ, the peasants had scuttled in under the MGs, under the long-guns. The mangled shapes confirmed it. Crushed and bleeding children, sprinters who had dashed in upon the speeding tanks to tackle the well-protected overlapping wheels, to get at the massive toothed tracks. Horribly maimed, they lay screaming in pain and hatred. The dead, the lucky ones, sprawled behind the tanks as if they had been dropped like dung from the hulls. But they had done their work, choking the tracks with wire and scrap metal, until all that power and weight and thrust had been strangled, and the grinding, gasping objects were as helpless as beached whales.

Even before the Tigers had slowed, the crowd had fallen on them, smashing off the protruding muzzles of the MGs, stopping every aperture with handfuls of earth, with sand from the river bed, with the wire bolases, timber wedges and one lethal device that Buz could not have imagined in his wildest nightmares.

The plunger tubs and rubber tubes were veterinary aids, equipment intended for the doctoring of sick animals. The ingenuity of the partisans had turned them into vicious weapons. The half-gallon galvanized tubs had been filled with sulphuric acid distilled from old batteries, or with strong solutions of caustic soda. The handlers, women, wore heavy industrial gloves. The slender tubes were poked through any hole that could be found, the plungers pumped. Scalding liquid, sprayed into the faces of the panzer crews through slit visors and MG ports, would create havoc within the tanks. As the limber rubber smoked and dissolved, fresh tubes were uncoiled, thrust into the tubs and recharged. Inside the Tigers the poor sons-of-bitches must be swimming in corrosive liquid.

Now the two vanguard Tigers heaved and twitched, all real forward motion ceased. They had penetrated the pass but had gained only forty yards beyond the 'two mules in harness' gate in the rocks before the partisans fouled and dismembered them.

Buz watched a turret hatch snap open. A German hull-gunner thrust himself out, flesh as black as his tank suit. Wisps of smoke adhered to his clothing, and his hands, held aloft in a futile plea for mercy, steamed. Two women, motherly types in knitted brown coats and head-shawls, dragged the panzer backwards over the rim of the hatch and stabbed him again and again with reaping shears.

From the hatch of the second tank, the commander emerged, bearing an improvised flag of surrender, a silk scarf knotted to a radio aerial. He wagged it frantically until it was torn from his grasp and he was flung to the ground where six or eight children fell upon him, flailing at his head and body with the barbed-wire bolases until there was precious little left by which to identify the thing that had been an officer of the Waffen–SS.

Nina said, 'They do only what is done to them.'

'Yeah, sure,' Buz answered.

He glanced to his right, towards the crest. They were there already, three more tanks, deftly positioned and stationary, long-guns staggered. Massed along their flanks were the grenadiers.

He would have shouted a warning to the villagers but Nina prevented it, pulling at his arm.

'They hear nothing,' she said. 'Come, we must find Victor.'

Running hard, Russian and sergeant retreated along the side of the highway, hugging the snow bank.

They had barely passed the tanks before the stationary Tigers fired a first salvo. Buz didn't look round. He had the feeling that maybe the krauts had fitted 'burster' shells, containing phosphorus, or Amatols into the long-guns. It would be like hosing out an ants'-nest, only it would be fire, not water, and the ants were human.

He tried to close his ears to the screaming.

'There,' Nina pointed. 'Victor.'

The partisan wore a tall, sheepskin hat with earflaps, and a sheepskin overcoat buttoned to his knees. Wrapped over his shoulder was an ammo belt and he had a big German Luger in each hand. He was grinning, his eyes watery with smoke and his skin pocked with cordite.

'We got, we got. See, you see,' he bawled.

But when Buz vaulted over the baffle in front of the trench and hauled himself round, he saw fuck-all to cheer about, only burning tanks, the charred and blistered remains of peasants annealed to the metal, and bloody bodies strewn everywhere.

'Victor,' Nina tugged at the old man's sleeve. 'The men, where are the men?'

Prancing foolishly, the partisan cheered and waved as if he was witnessing a victory parade and not a massacre.

The trench had seven wounded men in it, plus one battered mortar which didn't appear to be operating.

Still standing on the bank by the old man's side, Nina yelled at him in Russian, but Victor brushed the woman aside. He had no time for women, for strangers. Buz wondered where the hell the old guy thought he was and what old war he was fighting in his mind. But Victor wasn't quite so crazy as all that. He remained blinkered to the hideous scenes directly before him, concentrating on the snow and smoke that hid the place where the timber gate had been, near the site of the Vickers emplacement.

Then Buz got it together. He saw how it was; three tanks, burning hulks though they were, effectively checked the Tigers' advance. Victor was waiting for the arrival of the foot-soldiers, panzer-grenadiers and Gebirgstruppen, waiting for them to come to him so that he could kill men and not mechanical monsters.

If there had been three or four hundred partisans lined up, yeah, Buz might have cheered a little too at this levelling of the odds. But seven wounded men and a busted mortar weren't going to hold the krauts for long. The Tigers would pulverise the summit of the highway using flame shells and MGs, anything that wouldn't crater the road too badly, then the sappers would chain the burned hulks and haul them out of there and dump them and have clearway again. And a message would be sent out to Adolf, saying that the pass at Baku-Ashran was breached and where were the paratroops and the Luftwaffe and didn't the Third Reich *need* the oilfields any more? And there was nothing, but nothing, Victor or Boris or any of the mad Ruskies could do about it since they didn't have fifty peasants to fling away on every German tank, and no armaments worth talking about.

Yeah, he had seen what the Russians did to the Germans. He needed no lesson in what the Germans would do to the Russians. Wholesale shootings and hangings. No mercy; no prisoners. And all for a stretch of miserable track in godforsaken mountains hundreds of miles from anywhere.

Victor had noticed him at last. Scowling, the old man was waving him away, waving him back.

Buz lifted his head and peered down the highway where it made its first dip into the Ganevis valley. The skis were like flags stuck in the snow. The lip of the second trench, fortified with earth-bags and four beamed sledges, bristled with rifles and Stings.

The stand.

Yep, the Safaryans' last stand.

Who the fuck had him cornered, Buz wondered, the krauts or the Ruskies?

'You come?' Nina asked.

It was a goddamned stupid question. Where the hell else would he go?

'Yeah, sure. I come.'

Buz had barely reached cover in the second trench when the krauts' last blitzkreig began. He didn't spare a thought for rescue now, for P.B. or Deacon or Nina Safaryan.

Squatting on his heels in the mud-stained snow, he wiped down the Vaughan shotgun with his sleeve and stuffed two red cartridges into the breech.

In ten minutes, maybe less, he figured he would be staring up some kraut's nostrils and the only friend that would stand by him then would be one with two barrels and a gut full of 12-bore shot.

Deacon's right shoulder struck the rock. The rope jerked and dragged him in a violent pendulum, half slung over, ripping skin from his cheekbone, jaw and brow. He kicked, prodding his boots to find purchase and had got himself – just – into a reasonably upright position when, forty feet above him and well to his right, the piton sprang out. It was not unexpected.

Blood flowed into his eyes, but the impact had been light and he was not dazed or concussed. All his senses were trebly sharp, had been so since the instant he had heard the sullen crack of the rock fin and felt himself peeling away from adhesion with the wall. The hemp rope had so much stretch in it that he might have been suspended from a rubber band, and when the piton came away and he plummeted downward once more he was more or less prepared. Straight fall he could have coped with, but the side belay complicated things. He breasted the sack on his chest against the rock, buffering, and started to kick and fling his body outward to brake the drag of the big swing.

The next piton, if memory served him, was backed by a natural spike and had one of the screw-type karibiners on it. It would surely take the strain. If it didn't, he would be plunged downward and would collide with the edge of the rib – and he didn't like to think about that.

Actually, he was in complete control of himself once more and when the hemp bit against the angle of the belay, and held, Deacon let his body go, did not tense himself to halt the counterswing. Provided that P.B. was secure, he would dangle nicely in line with the lowest level of blue dye marks, only a pitch above Safaryan and the big ledge.

But the hemp had more flex than he had supposed and he was flung out and jerked and flung again, twisted by the rope's torque. He could not bend at the hips or cock his legs into position to protect himself. He slammed into something, spun, and, with the waistloop almost slicing him in half, was yanked backwards and banged his skull on the rock.

Shouts became very, very loud, and the milky sky reddened.

Dazed, battered, Deacon saw the rock loom up, as if it was a black disc zooming out of the sky. He managed to raise his forearms, but not enough. He crunched straight into the blackness at full tilt, and became part of it.

In three years of service to King and country, P. B. McNair had witnessed the deaths of many good mates. He had acquired an attitude of skin-deep camaraderie that enabled him to endure without undue suffering the loss of men with whom he had lived for months on end and with whom he had shared all manner of hardships. But with Deacon it was different. In the past eighteen months or so the Scot, the Canadian and the young English officer had established a bond that went deeper than friendship. When the piece of rock broke off in the Deke's mitts and he shot backwards into the empty sky, P.B. was stunned by shock.

P.B. had never fallen, had never been with anyone who had fallen, had never experienced the tremendous, spine-snapping forces that ropes transmitted. For a long, sick moment – while Deacon was still in free fall – P.B. thought that it was all up, all over with Jeff, and came close to doing something that he had never done before; he panicked.

The slapping crack of the hempen safety line around Deacon's middle, and the fact that the downward plunge was suddenly arrested, brought P.B. out of shock a split second before the rope ripped through his gloved hands.

From lying limp and sodden, a passive thing, the rope became deadly and swift. P.B. watched the coil come alive, the slack, sluggish, inching loops charged with an electric life of their own. He accepted the weight of Deacon's first fall only just in time, fast enough, in the end, to skip into a braced position, resisting the temptation to cock the rope around his wrists – an error that would have cost him his hands – to catch the loop around the fleshy part of his forearms and feed it out through open palms, grabbing and checking by degrees. He was ill-prepared, though, for such an almighty tug. It was like being sucked into a vacuum cleaner. It almost had him off the stance. Scrabbling, he held firm while the shock went through him into the belay spikes, stiffening the ropes that held him in place until every hair on them stood up like a spear. Then the piton catapulted out and Deacon was going down and across the face of the wall, scraped and dragged like a lure.

The yaw increased until it was all P.B. could do to contain it. He had to slacken the rope or be whipped into space by the gigantic snatching fist of the swing.

For several seconds he lost sight of Deacon.

Safaryan was yelling from below. The safety rope around P.B.'s middle became dangerously taut. He prayed to God the bloody Russian clown wouldn't go to bits, start reeling in *his* line; that would have him stood out in mid-bloody-air like a gyroscope balanced on a wire.

But Safaryan didn't pressure the lower rope and Deacon was in view again and P.B. hadn't time to think of anything because the fuckin' climbing ropes were twisted like buggeration and he could see, just before it happened, how Jeff would corkscrew out of the pendulum and into the one fuckin' bulwark on the lower level of the face.

It happened.

The Deke caromed into the rock profile, and stopped. The ropes untwisted, spun him. His head struck the rock a couple of times and then it was over.

Jeff was hanging there like a side of pork on a butcher's hook, stiff and slack at the same time, revolving, deadweight, on the rope's end.

It was utterly still, except for the wind, for a minute.

Safaryan had stopped bawling. The only sound P.B. could hear was the throb of blood in his ears and the pounding of his heart.

'Christ!' he said.

It didn't occur to him that Deacon might be dead.

From the valley floor came the slamming sounds of the

Vickers AT gun. But P.B. had enough to think about without starting to worry about Buz. He was still holding Jeff, the weight broken at the karibiner. The climbing rope was shaped like a slanted triangle, while the safety rope ran straight to the hanging figure below.

P.B. was no longer confused.

He wrist-looped the climbing rope, hauled it back as much as he dared and took an extra turn around the belay.

He had no hardware left; it was all down there with Jeff.

Safaryan – perhaps the girl – was quick to master the logistics of the problem. Before P.B. could unscramble the tangle, Natasha was pressing up the first pitch from the ledge. She climbed on a free rope, for Safaryan still had P.B. on belay. Peering down, P.B. saw the Russian's chubby countenance upturned like a haggis on a plate.

'Hold, hold,' Safaryan yelled. 'She get Deacon. You take rope.'

P.B. scowled, then shouted, 'Aye, right.'

The girl climbed like a wisp of smoke purling up a lum. She was already at the point where her traverse out to Deacon would begin. As P.B. watched, she dipped and swung on to the open face. The kid would splice an extra fifty feet of rope on to Deacon's free line then cut the taut rope and leave Jeff hanging. She would guide him down while he, P.B., took the full weight. There would be twenty or thirty feet of side sway but he doubted if that would give a wee chimpanzee like Natasha much bother at all. The girl was terrific. Good with a rifle, she was great on the rock. In spite of himself, P.B. felt a sudden, warm affinity with her; she was nothin' like his sister after all.

Reaching Deacon, the girl stood out from the rock on scant holds, beautifully poised, while she worked with one hand on the splicing procedure; plain, bulky, double fisherman's knots, pulled tight with her teeth, tied the two ropes together. It was not, P.B. knew, a particularly safe procedure, but he trusted the girl to guide Jeff carefully into the drop position where the vertical strain would keep the knots secure.

'Hey, kid. How is he, then?'

The girl glanced up at him, nodding, then jabbered in Russian.

He had almost forgotten she was a foreigner; she was spunky enough to be Scottish.

Safaryan relayed the message. 'Okay. Okay. Captain okay.'

P.B. murmured, 'Thank Christ.'

Natasha cut the rope above Deacon with a shearing knife from a sheath in her bodice, then, using her body as an anchor, eased him foot by foot across the wall.

Deacon was stirring now, swimming back into consciousness. P.B. was scared Jeff might do something that would swing him away from the girl's grasp. But the girl was talking nineteen to the dozen, soothing the captain, patting and touching him with her free hand between each series of crabbing movements across the wide open wall.

P.B. did nothing to distract her and when she reached the corner of the face below he took a fresh half-turn on the ropes around his forearms and bedded the strap-like rope around his shoulders.

Fixed to the end of the safety rope she had toted up the route, Natasha descended in a three-bound abseil to land as light as a moth on the ledge.

Deacon was all his.

Surprisingly, the weight was less of a strain than the sudden snatching force of the fall. He lowered Jeff slowly and smoothly. He could not see the landing but felt the weight go from him and, shaking slightly, leaned back the moment he heard Safaryan's cry, 'We got.' Not for an instant did P.B. suppose that the struggle with Sokhara was done.

P.B. was still shaking. It wasn't that he was scared. He'd been on the narrow stance too long, that was all. The cold had seeped into him without his being aware of it. Now that Jeff was okay, P.B.'s attention focused on the cannon in the valley. He fancied he could see the blush of an oil fire way, way down through the snow mist. But maybe it was imagination. Whatever it was, it meant that the bloody krauts were hurling themselves into the gap and that Buz and the lassies were hard pressed.

Anxiously, P.B. glanced up at the high charges, all of which were intact. The copper lead from the explosives under the overhang was secured to a peg behind him but the second level settings were incomplete and the wire had snapped when Jeff fell. Peering to his right, P.B. could see the end of it sticking out like a cat's whisker.

If the girl could handle the bottom level, he decided, he would rewire and complete the slab.

Bloody old Boris had obviously had just the same notion for the kid was already climbing up again with rucksack on her back.

She tipped her sweet face up and gave the corporal a smile.

P.B. grinned in response.

'Hey,' he said, optimistically, 'you wouldn't happen to have a fag on you, eh?'

The girl did not understand. But it didn't matter. For the next half-hour P.B. was far too busy to smoke.

Extract from the War Diary of Generalmajor Eric Münke

Seated together in the rear seat of his armoured command car, Gord and I conferred. We had a picture now of Russian manpower and weaponry. It was exceedingly encouraging. I confess I tended to over-value the courage of the partisans. Not so Oberführer Gord. He had seen this sort of thing, and worse, many times in the past. His arrogance and faith in the effectiveness of heavy armour had been tempered by circumspection. Even he was willing to admit that it was the timely, if unexpected, arrival of the Luftwaffe that had really unlocked the door of Baku-Ashran.

'We must take advantage of it,' Gord declared, 'not be deterred by the paltry defences that remain.'

Those Russian peasants would fight until they died, with hayforks and pruning hooks if there was nothing else to hand, but plugging the gap and erecting barriers on the

174

summit would not be enough to stop us. For every Tiger
that the partisans successfully halted, we had two more.
Firepower would carry the day. Gord's policy now was one
of cautious persistence.

The British Vickers-Armstrong gun appeared to be the
only weapon of armour-piercing capability and it had been
swiftly eliminated by our concentrated attack. Mortars
entrenched in side-hill positions had had no effect upon our
tanks, though the phalanx of panzer-grenadiers suffered
some casualties from the shelling. We knew, however, that
the British were few in number and that reinforcements had
failed to materialize. The couple of hundred or so partisans
that remained were no match for soldiers of the Reich.
Gord was scornful of their massed attack upon our lead
tanks.

'It gathers the sheep for the slaughter,' he said.

In a half-hour, the Oberführer assured me, his Tigers
would be rolling unimpeded through the gap and would be
safely strung out in the Ganevis valley, and our support
trucks, personnel carriers and even field guns, perhaps, could
be drawn through the door.

With hours of daylight left, Gord would make twenty
miles or more towards the oil towns before dusk, secure
in the knowledge that the Russians had been so depleted
in defence of the pass that a strong leaguer would be
impregnable to sneak attacks. The partisans simply did
not have the manpower to harry us further. Surveying the
multitude of corpses that had been flung to the side
of the highway – only two SAS men among them – I had
to agree with the Oberführer, though my optimism of Thursday
had been crushed by bloodshed and loss of so many
of my lads.

Gord smoked, and drank cold coffee from a metal bottle.
He held in his lap the box of the field telephone, which
connected him with front units, five hundred yards
ahead. His face was ivory white, hollowed by fatigue. He
had developed a crop of cold-sores at the corner of his

*mouth. None of it seemed to matter to him, not the snow
or the icy wind or the noise, not the smoke and fire
or even the wounded panzers that passed us, stretcher
cases being ferried back down to the trucks. In reaching
the summit of the pass, Oberführer Gord had fulfilled
himself. He had justified his rank and upheld the glory of
the Waffen-SS. He had earned the right to be a conqueror.*

*Candidly I had little stomach for glory, for conquest of
that order. I had only forty-seven men left and could not
put out of my mind the fact that, inevitably, we would have
to abandon most of our wounded, leave them to the mercy
of the Red Army. By this time tomorrow, unless all the
Führer's promises were kept, we would be running short
of fuel. The platoon trucks would be sacrificed to keep
the Tigers rolling. But victory and defeat are divided
by a line so thin that it is often invisible and I voiced no
disapproval of Gord's plans and kept my doubts to myself.*

'What would you have me do, Gord?' I asked.

*When he cast his gaze upon me I could tell that he
despised me. It came as no particular surprise but the
inference that the boys of the Gebirgsjäger 88 had
somehow failed him, stung.*

'Bring up the rear, Münke,' he said.

*I waited for him to add comment, a barbed remark, but
he lifted the receiver of the field telephone once more
and, by that action, excluded me from a share in command.*

I climbed out of the car and saluted Gord's uniform.

Perfunctorily he returned my salute.

*Turning, I trudged back down the highway, accompanied
by three officers and my signaller, dodging between Tigers
and trucks until we reached the sorry handful of Jäger
that remained.*

I did not let my annoyance show.

*We had a job to do and we would do it, even if
we had been swept into the background away from the
hard fighting.*

I split the ranks into three units and attached

one unit to each of the trucks. We were carrying most of
our equipment, packs and snow-shovels and ropes as well
as guns, and most of the lads had their skis strapped to
their backs. Our duty now was to keep the trucks from
bogging down, ensure that the column kept moving.

For the Gebirgsjäger it was a humiliation.

I joined my troops, on foot, at the rear of the
column as it clanked and growled and closed up into
the throat of the high pass. I cheered and chivvied them
along, my forty-seven brave lads who, because a stubborn
Oberführer thought them cowards, survived the fall of the
mountain.

Deacon's head had stopped bleeding. His vision had cleared
and his balance returned. Groggily he raised himself to his feet
and, grinning, offered to go up to help the climbers.

'*You mad,*' Safaryan shouted.

'Not that mad,' Deacon said. 'Joke – in poor taste.'

Deacon's head wound had been bound with shirting and his
mauled cheek and jaw cleaned with snow until the bleeding had
stopped. He looked like hell, with the clumsy bandage wrapped
round his head like a turban, and dried blood staining his
anorak.

Under the circumstances, though, he didn't feel too bad at
all. Having survived the fall, he felt quite light and elated, as
a matter of fact. He gave P.B. a feeble cheer as the Scot picked
his way down the slab and descended to the ledge, the end of
the lead wire tied firmly to his wrist.

'Christ!' said P.B. 'Y'look like ma old man after a night on
the wine. How d'you feel?'

'Dreadful,' said Deacon, grinning still.

The girl had finished before the corporal. She had completed
the setting and wiring of four charges in twenty minutes.

'You fit t'get off?' P.B. asked.

'Yes, but I'd better be roped tight,' said Deacon.

The girl took the wire and fed it along the ledge. Unroped,
she continued across the exposed traverse, running the wire

through the links that Deacon had set for it. She passed out of sight around the corner but returned, seconds later, to inform the colonel that the wire would not reach down into the gully.

Safaryan cursed in Russian.

'Why don't you bring the detonator charge box up on to the snow comb?' Deacon suggested.

'It will be dangerous, extreme.'

'Oh, everything's dangerous, Boris,' Deacon said. 'It's our only choice. It's that or abort the whole—'

'We do, we do.'

'If we hang a rope in the right place,' said P.B., 'I can hit the plunger and be over into the gully afore y'can say Piss Off.'

Using the ropes to keep both Safaryan and Deacon secure, the Scot and the Russian girl belayed them across the difficult traverse.

Deacon was weaker than he had supposed; loss of blood in a cold climate, perhaps, was the reason for it. He did not quite have command of his limbs and was possessed by a strange, floating sensation which did not contribute towards sound climbing.

Somehow, though, he was able to coax his way across the open part of the face and around the corner into the spur of the gully. The coxcomb of snow seemed to have grown much larger in the last hour and nuzzled against Deacon's hips and shoulders as he tottered down the rib and, on a fixed rope, lowered himself gingerly, with P.B.'s aid, into the gully bed.

At length the captain, the colonel and the girl were stationed in the gully, P.B. forty feet above them, just visible on the comb of snow. He had fitted the lead and wired it securely into the charger and had bedded the dark green metal box firmly in the snow. Behind him was a length of rope tied on to a rock spike.

'Ready?'

'Wait. We have sent no signal,' Safaryan said.

P.B. removed his fingers from the wooden handle of the plunger.

178

'Well, what's it goin' t'be? Now or later?' he called.

Deacon said, 'It's your decision, colonel.'

Safaryan tugged at his earlobe and stared down the gully into the snow cloud. The gunfire had all but ceased and the faint suspirations of machine-guns and rifles and the movement of tanks was so woven into the moaning of the winds of the mountain that it was impossible to judge the state of the battle.

Deacon consulted his wristwatch.

'We've been up here for three hours now,' he said.

'Five minutes take me down. I warn,' Safaryan nodded. 'Yes, it is me to warn.'

P.B. shouted, 'Hurry up. I'm bloody freezin'.'

Safaryan had already reached for his skis. 'I warn.'

'We won't be able to see a flare through this rubbish,' said Deacon. 'How will we know when you've reached the pass?'

'No need know.' The colonel snapped the clips on his boots and buckled the straps. 'Five minutes. Push. Boom!'

'Christ!' said P.B. loudly from the snow comb. 'Push! Boom!'

Deacon might have argued but Safaryan had already turned into the fall-line and, thrusting with his poles, had projected himself forward into the run. The girl cried after him but Boris Safaryan was out of earshot, swooping down the steep and icy runnel at an incredible rate.

'He'll never bloody make it,' P.B. announced.

Snow mist swallowed up the colonel.

Shakily, Deacon seated himself and put on his skis. There was no saying quite what would happen when the charges were detonated. Perhaps nothing of any consequence; a few stones skipping harmlessly down into the cloud. Perhaps a very great deal. Vibration alone might cause the whole face to shift. After all, Sokhara *was* a slag heap. The side buttress slanted away from the gully only three or four hundred feet above. He could understand now why the colonel had insisted that they travel with skis.

Deacon finished the strapping and got to his feet.

The girl too had equipped herself for a rapid descent. That only left P.B., stuck up by the comb.

Deacon's watch told him that time was up.

He lifted his ski-stick and prodded Natasha, urging her into the centre of the gully. The girl hesitated. Deacon whacked her across the seat with the flat of the stick and she flung herself round and drove downward, squatting into the line.

'You an' all, Jeff,' P.B. shouted. 'Get goin'.'

'No, I'll wait for you.'

'You an' me both know what's liable t'happen. I'll be better off without you t'look after. Get bloody goin'.'

Deacon stood his ground. 'Hit the button, wee man.'

'Shit!' said P.B. 'Have it your way, then.'

He vanished behind the crest of the snow comb.

A second later, the long, strong, slow rumble of explosion sounded around the mountainside, like heavy surf in a huge sea-cave.

P.B. leapt into view again, slithered down the hanging rope into the gully and dived for his skis.

Balanced on the sticks, Deacon cocked his head, staring in wonder up and around him as the surf-like surge continued, growing gradually louder. Nothing else seemed to be happening, though. Then a spray of snow and small stones detached from the buttress above and dribbled down into the gully.

Dear God, is that it? Deacon thought. Is that all the reward we get for so much risk and effort?

Then he saw the buttress, the whole damned thing, break out from the side of the gully, like the blade of a clasp-knife; an intact pillar of rock leaning further and further outwards.

'Oh, my God!' Deacon whispered.

P.B. stamped his boots into the ski clips, rose and shouted.

Deacon didn't hear him.

The pillar of rock was horizontal now, the first shattered rocks dropping from it like leaden rain, pattering and skittering into the gully bed. At the same instant, to Deacon's right, the sky was rent by the loudest sound that the captain had ever heard. He blinked in disbelief as he watched the entire northwest face of Sokhara shift, hang and begin to slide.

P.B. was shrieking at him but Deacon, entranced by the

spectacle, the mammoth destruction of the mountain, remained frozen to the gully bed.

The Scot pushed him, flailed at him with the ski-sticks.

Then the pillar broke and bent into the bed of the gully and danger overwhelmed awe.

Whipping round, Deacon slipped into a racing crouch, flexing and thrusting his thighs, and fled. P.B. was only a yard or two behind him, and the great wave of rock and ice only two or three hundred yards behind the Scot.

Buz held Nina by the nape of her neck and shouted into her ear, 'The crafty sonsabitches are saving the tanks. They're sending in their infantry.'

Nina screamed back at him but he could not understand her. In her excitement she spoke Russian.

Buz hefted the shotgun. He looked along the trench at Nina's girls, men in ragged uniforms, armed with Stings and carbines, and four or five good rifles. Up ahead, through the smoke, a few survivors of the tank attacks were limping towards him. He let the woman go, leaned his belly on the slant of the trench and squinted between the sled and the shoulders of a dead gunner. The Germans were a hundred yards away, packed under the defences that remained at the summit. He could just make out the Tigers behind the lines of grenadiers, their long-guns quiet now and, even as he watched, the hull guns falling still.

So the rush would come at any moment.

He stuck the stock of the Vaughan under his armpit and wiped his gloves carefully on his blouse.

Off to his right, two horses, mad with terror, galloped and reared and tore away up the steep, smooth snow slope that lay at the delta of the gullies that fanned down from Sokhara.

How long had Jeff and the crazy colonel been gone? Three hours, four? Buz had lost connection with time. The waiting periods and the hot, intense bouts of fighting had upset his perspective; it always happened. He should have hung on to the Vickers longer than he did, though, for sure.

Punctuated by sporadic shots between the trench and the

pack of krauts, the lull continued. Nobody was squandering heavy stuff any more, not even the Germans.

Nina was by him. He could smell her, a musky aroma of perspiration and damp blonde hair mingled with the Balkan cigarettes. She was breathing through her nose like a nervous mare. Buz put out his left hand, groped and found her hand and held it, squeezed it. She squeezed back but didn't look at him. She was transfixed by the sight of the krauts, by the metallic threat of the tanks tucked under the crest and the knowledge, maybe, that fifteen more Tigers were crouched just out of sight, their engines hot and their crews hotter, waiting to surge forward and claim possession of the pass.

The snow had stopped and the air seemed to sag like a wet, felt blanket.

The woman muttered something in her own tongue. Sounded like she was urging the Germans on, begging them to come, to break the nerve-wracking spell of waiting.

There were so many other noises that Buz's senses made nothing of the sound at first. It was so light, so out of place though, that the sergeant was first of all the people in the trench to recognize it.

He rolled on to his elbow, raising himself a little. Bullets whined thinly in the air but Buz paid them no heed.

He had heard that ridiculous friggin' racket somewhere else, back in the Lebanon, on another mountain, bollock-deep in a different kind of trouble, a different kind of snow.

Close to the place where the horses had bolted into the hanging mist, there was a figure, a guy on skis, rocketing out of the delta of the gullies like his ass was on fire.

And he was yelling. Nope, not yelling.

Yodelling.

Yodelling like a friggin' Swiss Miss with a mouth full of milk chocolate.

'Bloody Boris!' Campbell said aloud.

Nina had spotted her brother too.

Buz paid no further attention to the skier. He needed no more warning than the sight of the man.

The mountain was about to blow. And the krauts were in the clear. The lull had crapped up the plan. No matter how much or how little came down the mountainside, the remaining partisans would take the brunt of it, not the panzers.

'Nina, get them out. Fall back. For Christ's sake, fall back!'

The blonde understood perfectly.

Screaming at the pitch of her voice, she leapt to her feet and scrambled over the bed of the trench and up the rear slope, falling, picking herself up again. She waved and screamed and her girls, the handful left of the Angels of Death, obeyed her without question. They went up like lizards and ran, some with skis, some with rifles.

Buz stood, gesturing, shouting.

Puzzled, the partisans in the trench did nothing.

Boris Safaryan was being drawn away by the contours of the hill. It would be ten minutes before the colonel could track back to them. He would hit the highway a half-mile east in the Ganevis valley.

Then there was Victor, the old man, prancing and bawling at Buz, and Buz bawling back. He caught the old man by the lapels and shook him and flung him down, and lifted him again and flung him bodily up the slope. Victor scrabbled and clawed his way to the top of the trench, his face twisted with hatred. He lifted the Luger and aimed it straight into the Canadian's face.

Arms spread, Buz waited to be shot.

But it was Victor who collected the bullet, the first bullet of the panzer charge. He fell backwards, straight and stiff as a cord of wood, and the rest of the Russians who, a moment before, had been bewildered and confused, fled as one for the chasm's protective shoulder.

Buz ran, then halted, stooping. He swivelled. Every man, woman and child in the partisan army was retreating now, streaming back from the trenches, spreading outward on to the snow banks or plunging down into the bowl of the river.

More important, the panzer-grenadiers were advancing at the

double, firing as they came. And behind them, the first pair of tanks debouched out of the mouth of the pass and charged down the broadening highway, increasing speed with every yard. The krauts had swallowed the bait. Two more Tigers, then four, then six – snouts to tails they claimed the vacated ground, grinding over corpses and battering down puny staves, rolling over slit trenches.

Nina grabbed Buz and hauled him over the edge of the river slope, but he stayed her, pulling her in turn down by him.

'Now, Boris, for Chrissake. Where is it?' Buz yelled.

As if in answer to his question, the layer of mist above the pass quivered and emitted a profound bass growl – like, Buz thought, the voice of God.

The growl was sustained, steady for a while, then growing swiftly in volume, in resonance, until the sergeant felt it vibrate in every cell in his body. At first it was eerie, then it became terrifying, like he imagined an earthquake might be, only worse because there was no visible sign of earth movement. Even though he knew what caused it, Buz was scared. To the krauts, who had no explanation, the crescendo of noise must be enough to strike dread into their hearts. Tank drivers, gunners, grenadiers, sappers, platoon commanders and high brass, none would be immune.

Buz watched the tanks slow down, the first avid thrust checked, not by guns or shells but by that all-enveloping sound.

'Look,' Nina cried. 'Another one.'

Buz followed the line of her pointing finger.

A second skier had emerged from the cloud skirts. Travelling faster than Safaryan, the figure veered left, tracing a route parallel with the highway but three or four hundred feet higher up, where the snow sloped gently.

'It is Natasha.'

'Where the friggin' hell are Deacon and P.B.?' Buz demanded.

'Wait. See.'

The sound was breaking up – Buz could identify it, though he hadn't heard its like before and never would again – breaking into a great vomit of rock and snow, as hundreds of thousands

184

of tons of the stuff poured out of kilted, grey cloud. Two figures rode before it; Deacon and the wee man, skiing for dear life, skiing so fast they were almost on the wing, shoved on, maybe, by the bow-wave of the gargantuan landslide.

Buz's gaze did not leave the pair until they had zigzagged left and were out of the fall line, pursuing the girl, Natasha, and Safaryan far down the contour of the valley.

When Nina hauled at him again, this time he needed no urging.

They kneed themselves back on to the edge of the highway and ran like hares, east towards the plain, out of the track of the lava-like downpouring which engulfed everything in its path.

Nina's girls and many of the partisans were with them, all sprinting, bug-eyed, straining to put themselves beyond the reach of the rock tide.

Then Nina stumbled and fell. Buz braked and turned, darted back for her, saw that they were out of danger and, in awe, remained rooted, kneeling by the woman's side, to watch the death of the German armoured column and the sealing of the pass.

Not in his wildest dreams could the Red colonel have envisaged such total devastation, such an unleashing of force. Half a mountain fell like an ocean out of the lagged sky, gathering volume and momentum, deluged the pass and the highway around it over a half-mile stretch, and choked on its own mass in the chasm.

Buz had no notion of how many tanks were trapped in the area of fall. Twelve at least, he figured. He saw two, the advance guard, consumed by tongues of rock, pushed over as if they were made of matchwood, crushed and buried, all in the space of five seconds. He saw running men, grenadiers, lifted and borne away on the jagged current. And a German command car, like a kiddie's toy, riding on top of the flow, two SS officers in it, their arms raised helplessly in pointless surrender. The car was still upright, the officers alive, when the stone sea smashed down into the chasm, taking them along with it to bury them for ever on the river bed.

And when, in six or seven minutes, it was over and only the last dribbles of snow dust trickled down, there was a silence like that of a tomb, a silence without shot or cry to disrupt it. The whole shape of the mountain pass had been changed. There was no more Baku-Ashran, no shoulder, no chasm, no gap, only settling shoals of the debris that, for tens of thousands of years, had formed the north-west face of Mount Sokhara.

Nina climbed to her feet and, trembling, clung to him.

Softly stroking her hair, Buz held her.

It was all over.

Sure, there would be mopping up, wounded to take care of and the krauts' remaining trucks to be pillaged. He didn't doubt that bloody Boris would be skiing up the track as fast as his stout little legs could carry him, hog-calling the survivors to gather round, organizing the partisans and Angels of Death into raiding bands to fall upon and eliminate the tail of the German column.

No prisoners, no mercy?

Maybe Boris would be so chuffed at the success of his grand plan that he would change his mind about slaughtering everybody in a German uniform. With the Red Army only a day's march away, Buz figured that Boris would preserve enough prisoners to put on a big parade. From what he had heard of Russian POW camps, though, the poor sonsabitches might be better off dead.

P.B. and Jeff were alive, and that was all that really mattered to him. In a day or two or three Deacon would bully Safaryan into finding transport to get them to a railhead or an airfield or maybe back down the highway to Baku or one of the other oil towns, to ferry them out of the Caucasus and back to the regiment, back home to the desert.

As far as Buz was concerned his piece of the Russian war was over. The mailed fist had been chopped off at the wrist, the krauts wiped out, everything wiped out. There for nothing left to fight, nothing left to fight for. Buz felt strangely empty, and exhausted.

But not that exhausted.

For the next few days he would have Nina to console him.

Tonight, in the snug confines of the shepherds' hut or across the mountain in Dzera, somewhere, they would lie naked together and do more than talk, a whole lot more.

Rommel would just have to wait.

Buz held the woman closer while, billowing across the scarred mountainside, snow began to fall once more.